Michigan Classics in Chinese Studies

T0324389

THE TOWER
OF
MYRIAD MIRRORS

A Supplement to
Journey to the West

By Tung Yüeh (1620-1686)

Translated from the Chinese by
Shuen-fu Lin and *Larry J. Schulz*

CENTER FOR CHINESE STUDIES
THE UNIVERSITY OF MICHIGAN
ANN ARBOR

Michigan Classics in Chinese Studies
No. 1

Published by Center for Chinese Studies
The University of Michigan
Ann Arbor, Michigan 48109-1106

Second Edition 2000
© 2000 by Regents of the University of Michigan
All rights reserved

Printed and made in the United States of America

∞ The paper used in this publication meets the minimum requirements
of the American National Standard for Information Sciences—
Permanence of Paper for Publications and Documents
in Libraries and Archives ANSI/NISO/Z39.48—1992.

Library of Congress Cataloging-in-Publication Data

Tung Yüeh, 1620–1686
    [Hsi yu pu. English]
    The tower of myriad mirrors : a supplement to Journey to the West / by
Tung Yüeh ; translated from the Chinese by Shuen-fu Lin and Larry J. Schulz.
        p.   cm.   — (Michigan classics in Chinese studies ; no. 1)
        Originally published: Berkeley, Calif. : Asian Humanities Press, 1978.
        ISBN 0-89264-142-8 (alk paper)
        I. Lin, Shuen-fu, 1943– II. Schulz, Larry James. III. Wu, Ch'eng-en,
ca. 1500–ca. 1582. Hsi yu chi. IV. Title. V. Series.
    PL2698.T83 H713 2000
    895.1'348—dc21
                                                                    00-060228

        ISBN 978-0-89264-909-9 (electronic)

To Kathleen, Joanne, and Andrew;
Barbara and Daniel

CONTENTS

INTRODUCTION

It is customary to speak of six "great novels" as the most important long works of traditional Chinese vernacular fiction. Two of them, a picaresque and a historical romance called, respectively, *The Water Margin* (*Shui-hu chuan*) and *The Romance of the Three Kingdoms* (*San-kuo-chih yen-i*), come from the fifteenth century. Two more, *Journey to the West* (*Hsi-yu chi*), a fantasy travelogue, and *Chin P'ing Mei*, a pornographic work of social realism, are from the sixteenth century. The last two, the satiric *The Scholars* (*Ju-lin wai-shih*) and *Dream of the Red Chamber* (*Hung-lou meng*), a novel of upper-class manners, are eighteenth-century works. The isolation of these six works as "great novels" is largely justified in that most other traditional novels were imitative of them, so that each of the six may be said at once to typify and epitomize its own subgenre of fiction.

A Western reader acquainted with these works in translation might find that they fulfill in some limited ways his conception of the premodern novel—they develop the surface aspects of narrative and characterization in order to tell a story that proceeds sequentially from one event to the next. Not unexpectedly, he will miss in them the psychological exploration and willingness to experiment with form that has characterized Western fiction since Proust and Joyce.

The seventeenth-century novel here translated as *The Tower of Myriad Mirrors* was originally known as *Hsi-yu pu* in Chinese, literally "A Supplement to *Journey to the West*," a title that suggests it belongs to the subgenre of fantasy travelogues spawned by the success of *Journey*. Yet except for the appropriation of the original novel's characters and story frame, *The Tower of Myriad Mirrors* develops in directions that contrast sharply with the rest of early Chinese fiction, and in ways that are easily accessible to a modern reader versed in twentieth-century literature and its vocabulary.

1

One aspect of the present novel's uniqueness is its use of dream. Chinese writers traditionally used dream sequences to provide a middle plane between the human and supernatural worlds—several instances can be found in *Journey to the West*, as indicated in the summary of the novel below—or as a foil dramatizing the ephemeral quality of human life. In the latter case, a character experiences the vacillations of fate over an entire lifetime, suffering rise and decline in status, raising a family, and dying, only to awake and learn he had dreamed it all in seconds. In neither case is the logic of waking life suspended; there is merely a shift in setting that must be clearly marked if it is to be intelligible. By contrast, *The Tower of Myriad Mirrors* is cast entirely as the dream of its protagonist, Monkey. Only in the last chapter do Monkey and the reader learn that the action has unfolded in the world of dream.

The sense of dream here is evoked by the surreal logic familiar to dreamers. An image suggested in a previous context becomes concrete, like the inexplicable wall that materializes inside the gate of the Emerald Green World after the Sky-walkers have told Monkey about a wall built to sever the road to the West. The idea of the wall itself is associated with an earlier mention of the First Emperor of Ch'in, consolidator of China's Great Wall. Time becomes disjointed, changing without notice from abnormal speed, as when the Hsiang Yü story takes place in the course of a single night, to the extended analysis of a single moment, as in the description of Beautiful Lady Yü's morning toilet. Or there are such uncanny occurrences as the two instances when Monkey involuntarily enters the Tower of Myriad Mirrors, once by tripping on a stone and once by being pushed into a pool of water.

The treatment of dreams in *The Tower of Myriad Mirrors* goes beyond convincing description to an intuition of their psychological functions that anticipates the discoveries of modern psychology. Further, the use of dream is inseparable from the novel's Buddhist design. It may be said that the novel is equally penetrating as the recounting of Monkey's dream and as an exposition of the Buddhist, especially Ch'an (Zen), experience in terms of the unconscious mind, whose processes are revealed most graphically in dreams.

Equally unparalleled in Chinese fiction is the novel's structure, a succession of shifting perspectives that matches the fluctuating settings and time planes of the dreamscape. It starts off properly enough in the storyteller mold inherited from *Journey to the West*, but shortly the sense of reality begins to fragment, and the story is propelled through the bits and pieces of a narrative montage. First there is the concubine's monologue, which after a descriptive interlude introduces the Mountain-removing Bell. Then there is a reading from a dynastic history and the Sky-walker's speech, both of which contain jolting revelations for Monkey. Disparate devices are used as the novel proceeds, among them Hsiang Yü's autobiographical tale, the head workman's bill of accounts, and the song of the blind singing girls, which recounts history from its mythological beginnings through dynastic times and back again to the fabled pilgrimage of *Journey to the West*.

Monkey's return to waking life is marked by the observation that the sun has not moved from the peony tree whose appearance initially set the story in motion. True to the traditional function of dream in fiction, this critical and seemingly time-consuming event in Monkey's spiritual life has all taken place in a single moment. But this well-worn formula is used not because it is a convenient way to end the story, but to bring it back to the traditional format of *Journey to the West*, which, now rectified by the supplement, can move on to its own chapter sixty-two.

In this move the novelist exhibits the level of control over his medium that is characteristic of *The Tower of Myriad Mirrors* as a whole. It is made possible at least in part because Tung chose to abandon the unwieldy length favored by his predecessors. He also chose to dispense with another fixture of earlier novels, the conventional storyteller line: "And if you want to know what happened, read the next chapter." This phrase is only used once—in chapter twelve, which builds from a narrative told in the storyteller fashion. Absent, too, are the poems inserted at battle scenes or at each passage calling for natural description, typical of novels like *Journey to the West*. Instead, description is largely confined to prose, and important settings such as the interior of the Tower of Myriad Mirrors are catalogued at length and with relish.

The Author

The author of *The Tower of Myriad Mirrors*, Tung Yüeh, (styled Jo-yü), was born in 1620. His birthplace, Nan-hsün in northern Chekiang, was across Lake T'ai from Soochow, then one of the great cultural centers of China. He was the grandson of a high official and son of a literatus who died when Tung was seven. The boy was raised an only child and passed the lowest level of the civil service examinations when he was seventeen, but apparently pursued government service no further. This was perhaps because the succession of corrupt and ineffective reigns that culminated in the destruction of the Ming court by the Manchu Ch'ing dynasty in 1644 made an official career unattractive; also perhaps because he found that preparation for the examinations, which he satirizes fiercely in *The Tower of Myriad Mirrors*, detracted from his more purely intellectual pursuits. He is known to have studied the *I Ching* (*Book of Changes*), with an eminent scholar of the subject named Huang Tao-chou.

Tung married and had several children, but at the age of thirty-six he accepted the Buddhist tonsure and entered a monastery. Not a few intellectuals of the day sought refuge in Buddhism from service to the Ch'ing dynasty and its insistence that Chinese clothing and hair styles be replaced by those of Manchu custom. Political considerations, however, seem not to have played a significant part in the decision of Tung Yüeh, who had been interested in Buddhism from an early age, and who went on to become a respected master of the Ch'an school. He died in 1686.

Tung's biographer, Liu Fu, lists more than one hundred titles attributable to him, testament to a broad range of interests spanning the Chinese classics, particularly the *Book of Changes*, ancient Chinese history, belles-lettres, Buddhism, research in literary history, prosody, and dreams. His miscellaneous works deal with astronomy, chronology and the calendar, etymology of medicinal plant names, and the connoisseurship of incense. They also include one novel, *The Tower of Myriad Mirrors*. This diversity may reflect the restless temperament of a man who was given to changing his name frequently and who occasionally threatened to burn all his literary work.

Liu also discovered a poem of 1650 dating *The Tower of Myriad Mirrors* as a work of 1640, Tung Yüeh's twentieth year. This date tallies with the one given for a preface to the novel, and though critics have found it difficult to accept that a first and only novel should have achieved such depth and technical mastery, there is no documentation to counter the poem's implication that *The Tower of Myriad Mirrors* is the product of a remarkably precocious mind.

The Setting: JOURNEY TO THE WEST

Since *The Tower of Myriad Mirrors* purports to supplement the earlier novel *Journey to the West* by inserting its sixteen chapters between chapters sixty-one and sixty-two of the original, it behooves us to know something of that novel, and especially the episode that generated the supplement. *Journey to the West* evolved from a story cycle based on the pilgrimage to India made by the T'ang dynasty cleric Hsüan-tsang (A.D. 602–664) in search of authentic Buddhist texts. Wu Ch'eng-en (ca. A.D. 1500–1580) put it into its present form, wherein Hsüan-tsang's role has become secondary to that of his heroic disciple, Sun Wu-k'ung, or Monkey. The story line no longer recounts the often lonely journey across Central Asia, but a fabulous adventure guided unerringly by its mission, with supernatural assistance, through lands ruled by monsters and demons. It is, as has often been pointed out, a kind of *Pilgrim's Progress* toward Buddhist salvation.

Sun Wu-k'ung is a stone monkey born from a stone egg. After establishing himself as monkey king at Water-curtain Cave in the Mountain of Flowers and Fruit, he one day realizes that he, like other mortal creatures, is destined to die and sets out to see what can be done about it. He receives training in techniques of longevity and physical transformation from the Taoist Patriarch Subodhi. Returning home, he bullies the Dragon King of the Eastern Sea into giving him an enchanted cudgel that becomes his trademark and with which he later harrows Hell in a dream. These acts bring him to the attention of Heaven's Jade Emperor, who, rather than do battle with him, gives Monkey the sinecure of Groom to the Heavenly Stables. As soon as he discovers how low his status is, Monkey goes home and fights a punitive heavenly army to a stalemate, winning as a concession the title Great Sage Equal of Heaven. But soon he takes offense at being excluded from a banquet and again leaves Heaven—but not before imbibing great quantities of banquet wine and some of Lao-tzu's elixir of immortality.

The full forces of Heaven, aided by the magic of the Bodhisattva Kuan-yin, capture Monkey after a tremendous battle, but no way can be found to dispose of him. Even the alchemical fires of Lao-tzu's Eight Trigram Cauldron fail, and Monkey is able to escape, change into a six-armed, three-headed apparition brandishing three cudgels, and go on a rampage that threatens to bring down the throne of Heaven. Finally, Buddha is called upon and proposes that if Monkey can but jump off the palm of His hand, he can be king of Heaven. Of course, the Buddha's magic proves more powerful, and Monkey is cast down beneath Five Phases Mountain, there to do penance and await the coming of Hsüan-tsang.

The story then skips ahead five hundred years to tell of Hsüan-tsang's miraculous youth. It gives an account of the T'ang emperor T'ai-tsung's dream trip to the Underworld and his plans for an elaborate mass for the dead to be said in thanksgiving for his safe return. The pious Hsüan-tsang is chosen to officiate and, at the suggestion of the disguised Kuan-yin, is entrusted to go to India in search of scriptures that will introduce Mahayana Buddhism to China. After a royal send-off, the pilgrimage is immediately beset by monsters. Hsüan-tsang watches as his several disciples are eaten but is saved himself by the Spirit of the Planet Venus and takes shelter in the house of the hunter Liu Po-ch'in. Liu accompanies him to the border of China and Five Phases Mountain, where Monkey is released from the Buddha's spell and becomes Hsüan-tsang's chief disciple. After killing the Six Thieves in defense of Hsüan-tsang, however, Monkey takes offense at his new master's scolding for taking life and runs off. Kuan-yin persuades him to return, and in the meantime has given Hsüan-tsang a flowered cap inlaid with gold as a means of disciplining Monkey. Once donned, the cap cannot be removed and contracts painfully whenever Hsüan-tsang intones a certain charm. Monkey, in agony, tears off all but a golden hoop, which remains permanently fixed on his head.

The two, thus outfitted, continue on and acquire a white horse—a transformed dragon—for Hsüan-tsang to ride, and the disciples Pigsy and Sandy, both originally monsters who submit at Kuan-yin's urging after a fight with Monkey. Master and disciples proceed along the road to the West, encountering monster after monster. All are dispatched by the entourage's fighting skills or are converted to Buddhism through the intervention of Kuan-yin and other divinities. Eventually, after passing through the appointed eighty-one trials, they obtain the scriptures, then are whisked to China and back to the Buddha's Vulture Peak retreat. Monkey and Hsüan-tsang are made buddhas and the others, saints of lesser orders.

After its publication in 1596, *Journey to the West* was admired for both its story and its allegories of Buddhist and Taoist teachings. Tung Yüeh found in chapters fifty-nine through sixty-one an incident that inspired him to expand the original's scope in both aspects. In that episode, the pilgrims come to a very hot land where everything is scorched red. They are told that a flaming mountain, from which the area derives its name, changed the climate to eternal broiling summer. Monkey learns that Lady Rakshas possesses a Banana-leaf Fan capable of blowing out the flames and goes to her cave to ask for it. But because Monkey and Kuan-yin had earlier defeated her son, the Red Boy, Monkey instead must face the fan in battle. He loses the first round and is blown thousands of miles away—right to the abode of a bodhisattva from whom he receives a wind-resistant staff and heaviness pills. Now able to withstand Lady Rakshas' assaults, he forces her into her cave, then changes into an insect and enters her belly. There he rampages until she is tortured into surrendering the fan. When he attempts to put out the flaming mountain, however, the flames only leap higher, and the local tutelary deity informs him he has been deceived by a fake fan. What's more, he learns that it was he himself who started the fire when he tipped over the Eight Trigram Cauldron some five hundred years earlier.

Monkey decides to use his sworn brotherhood with the Demon Bull King, Lady Rakshas' estranged husband, to capture the real fan. As before, though, he confronts an adversary incensed over the Red Boy matter. They fight until the Bull King retires from the field. Monkey assumes the Bull King's form, steals his chariot, and calls on Lady Rakshas. Hoping to lure her "husband" away from his mistress and back home for good, she brings out wine and attempts to seduce him. Monkey plays along to the extent of drinking with her, then turns the conversation to the fan and suggests she give it to him for safekeeping. Once he has it, he returns to his own form and leaves. The Demon Bull King, realizing what has happened, changes into Pigsy and tricks Monkey into giving back the fan. But he cannot fan Monkey away, due to the heaviness pills, and the fight is on again. It rages until Monkey and the real Pigsy smash into Lady Rakshas' cave.

The Bull King tries to flee but finds himself cut off in all directions by Buddhist and Taoist deities; he is finally led away with a rope through his nose. The story ends well: The fire is put out and the proper ordering of the seasons returns to the land; the Bull King is led back to the Buddha land, and a reformed Lady Rakshas asks that the fan be returned to her. This Monkey does reluctantly, and the pilgrimage continues westward.

Interpretations of THE TOWER OF MYRIAD MIRRORS

The flaming mountain story typifies Wu Ch'eng-en's method of handling obstacles encountered on the pilgrimage. A crisis occurs, Hsüan-tsang is helpless, and so Monkey takes over and battles whatever monster is responsible, until, often with divine aid, the fight is won. Thus, as Tung Yüeh's "Answers to Questions" preface (see Appendix) states, Monkey's first recourse is always his superior power. He deals only with the external surface of each situation, and in an almost mechanical manner. This makes sense in the context of *Journey to the West,* whose intention is to show Monkey's submission—the submission of the self-inflated will—to the discipline that alone can lead to salvation. That is, going to visit Buddha presents no problem to one with Monkey's powers, but being bound to accompany a bumbling priest on an overland route beset with frustrations is an allegorical environment wherein Monkey can acquire self-control and self-consciousness.

This process remains unarticulated in the novel itself, which shows no change in Monkey's character, even after he has been awarded buddhahood. The interest in him as a fantastic hero and in the invention of monsters for him to fight wins out over subtlety in characterization, and we are left to believe that Wu Ch'eng-en's Monkey becomes a buddha simply because he has completed a physical quest.

Finding this conclusion inadequate, Tung Yüeh decided to patch *Journey to the West* with a sequence probing the internal workings of Monkey's mind. He chose for his vehicle a hallucinatory world evoked by the demon of desire, called Ch'ing Fish, which is a purely yin force proportionate to Monkey's inherent yang. Following from this, a sense of antithesis informs the major imagery of *The Tower of Myriad Mirrors.* From the Land of Flaming Mountain, where everything is red and unaffected by the change of seasons, the pilgrims have "come again to the land of green spring." But an echo of the former redness, the peony tree, signals Monkey's absorption into dream, and events that fly in the face of what he recognizes as reality soon begin to occur.

Reversals of reality are concretized in the many mirrors of the Tower. Monkey enters one mirror and becomes Beautiful Lady Yü, his sexual opposite. The orderly perception of time is eroded by the discovery of three coexisting levels of time beyond the normal: a World of the Ancients, a World of the Future, and a World of Oblivion. When Monkey presides in the World of the Future, he reads a calendar that runs backward from the end of the month to the beginning. And opposition becomes oxymoron when he meets the New Ancient, the original time-traveler who helps Monkey back into the Tower.

From a Buddhist point of view, all this is necessary to undercut Monkey's assumption that the information provided by his senses can be trusted with the degree of confidence he exuded during the earlier part of the pilgrimage. The Tower of Myriad Mirrors stands as the central image in this process, a key to multiple planes of existence beyond Monkey's imagination. As such, it has a parallel in the *Avataṁsaka Sūtra*. There the Bodhisattva Maitreya creates for one Sudhana a spiritual aid, a tower that holds a self-contained cosmos. Within the tower are arrayed countless similar towers, each with its own cosmos and each of those with a Maitreya and a Sudhana. Sudhana sees all time in one glance and is enlightened.

When Monkey attempts to leave the Tower, he becomes enmeshed in red threads—recalling once again the Flaming Mountain—but is extricated by an old man who snaps the threads one by one. This is a turning point because the old man is Monkey himself, and he has therefore effected a meeting between the deluded, pre-enlightened self and that deeper self, which by the tenets of Mahayana Buddhism is always enlightened. After Monkey leaves the Tower he is, like his counterpart Sudhana, on the way to spiritual awakening.

From the standpoint of both Buddhist and modern dream psychology, the Tower segment may be said to take place in the depths of the unconscious, to represent a fundamental reordering of Monkey's psyche carried out in a setting complementary to waking life. It leaves unresolved, however, the disorders of his unconscious accumulated at the Flaming Mountain—namely, the sexual desire implied by Monkey's penetration of Lady Rakshas' body and his penchant for relying on his physical strength. These two themes run persistently through *Tower*. Sexual innuendo abounds at a party with the lady Green Pearl, and quite specifically in Monkey's poetic line, "I regret that my heart follows clouds and rain in flight." "Clouds and rain" is a timeworn literary euphemism for sex. As Beautiful Lady Yü, Monkey tries to avoid bedding with the warrior Hsiang Yü, but this episode and others recall the scene in *Journey to the West* where Monkey drinks shoulder-to-shoulder with Lady Rakshas. When the enraged Monkey beats a little monkey[1] who has reported how he met a young girl and got drunk with her, he is plainly punishing himself.

In another projection of the Lady Rakshas "affair," King Pāramitā explains that he is the son of Monkey and Lady Rakshas, and Monkey becomes aligned against his own offspring in the chaotic Battle of the Banners. As the climax of the novel, this battle is in keeping with Ch'an essentials, which teach that when one's perplexity reaches its highest pitch, psychic energies have become concentrated enough to thrust one into new awareness.

This same battle is the culmination of the recourse-to-strength theme as well, for Monkey again assumes the three-headed, six-armed form he used in his rebellion against Heaven. Monkey likes to rely on massive response, and this is why he looks to weapons like the Mountain-removing Bell and the Banana-leaf Fan rather than working through the subtler nuances of his predicaments. Such devices would make the westward journey easy and allow Monkey to avoid the very trials that give the allegorical pilgrimage its meaning. Ultimately, Monkey is not required to abandon his use of force, but to ensure that it is steered toward attaining Buddhist objectives. The story ends, after all, with his smashing of the Ch'ing Fish demon in its guise of a young acolyte who has offered to follow the pilgrims to the West. His act of striking down the acolyte "without a second thought" is an example of intuitively appropriate action in the Ch'an sense. The Ch'ing Fish is Monkey's mirror image—born at the same time and as evil as Monkey is good—so slaying this demon emancipates Monkey's mind from the grip of illusion. It is a violent act, but as Tung Yüeh notes in his "Answers to Questions" (see Appendix), "In killing the demon of desire, one must be prepared to cut it in half with one stroke."

If a Buddhist reading of *The Tower of Myriad Mirrors* seems most consonant with the author's overt design, there is also a school of

---

[1] Little monkeys are assistants Monkey magically summons by chewing his fur into bits and then blowing them out.

interpretation comprised of such modern Chinese critics as Liu Ta-chieh and Han Chüeh, who view the novel as a disguised attack on the alien Manchus and the Chinese who served them. They insist that Ch'ing Fish, the key demon in the story, is meant to call to mind the name of the Manchu dynasty rather than the homophone that means "desire." Though this reading relies upon the probably erroneous belief that the novel was written in retrospect of the Manchu seizure of China, it suggests noteworthy possibilities for interpretation.

The first name Nurhachi chose for his Manchu dynasty was Later Chin, adopted in 1616. Tung Yüeh may well have had this name in mind when he depicted the interrogation and torture of Ch'in Kuei, a man popularly believed to have sold out the twelfth-century Sung court in favor of the first Chin dynasty, which was, like the Manchu court, of non-Han origin. The Manchus changed their dynastic title to Ch'ing in 1636, so that if the novel were indeed written in 1640, the Ch'ing dynasty might well be imbedded in the Ch'ing Fish. In this light it is significant that a smell that offends Monkey when he meets the New Ancient in Shantung Province comes from the Tartars "right next door." If the Manchus were still in their homeland, "next door" to the north, then invasion remained at least an ominous prospect, though not an accomplished fact.

There is a sense of urgency in the New Ancient's warning that Monkey's whole body will take on the smell if he remains too long. Abhorrence of the polluting association between Chinese and barbarian is figured in Ch'in Kuei, who says pointedly, "There will be many Ch'in Kueis in the future—even today their number is not small." Possibly Tung Yüeh meant to challenge the complacency that led the court to underestimate the gravity of the Manchu threat, even on the eve of its destruction.

Because *The Tower of Myriad Mirrors* is open to more than one interpretation, we have attempted to be as unambiguous as possible with our translation. It is hoped that the footnotes and the foregoing introduction will provide the Western reader with at least an approximation of the knowledge that a Chinese reader would bring with him to the novel. To this extent we have explained allusions and puns that are not immediately obvious in translation. Certainly, the one great pun that hangs over the entire work is based on characters with the sound *ch'ing*, which may point simultaneously to desire, the color green, and the Ch'ing dynasty.

We have maintained the names Monkey, Pigsy, Sandy, and other incidental proper names coined by Arthur Waley in his *Monkey*, an abridged translation of *Journey to the West*. Following Tung Yüeh's preference, however, Hsüan-tsang is referred to as the T'ang Priest, rather than Tripitaka, as in *Monkey*.

In preparing this translation, we have followed the 1955 edition of the *Hsi-yu pu* published by Wen-hsüeh ku-chi k'an-hsing-she in Peking. This edition appends Liu Fu's sketch of Tung Yüeh's life and writings from which most of the biographical information in this introductory note has been drawn. The Shih-chieh shu-chü edition (Taipei, 1970) was also consulted.

Bringing Monkey, his master, and brother pilgrims into print again is like happening upon a fellow traveler from one's past—someone last seen through a wave of the hand in a Rangoon station or on a dusty street in Kaifeng. The road to the West takes many turns and, along with its trials, holds a few pleasant surprises. Thanks to the University of Michigan's Center for Chinese Studies, Shuen-fu Lin and I have renewed our acquaintance with *The Tower of Myriad Mirrors* and are pleased that new readers will be able to experience this unique narrative and its intricate web of imagery. We have taken advantage of this new edition to make a few changes in the introduction, and corrections as well as revisions to the body of the novel, under the insightful editorial eye of Terre Fisher. We are grateful to her for her guidance.

Larry J. Schulz
Atlanta, 2000

THE TOWER
OF
MYRIAD MIRRORS

CHAPTER ONE

As the Peonies Glow Red, the Ch'ing Fish Breathes Out Its Spell
Issuing an Elegy for the Wrongly Killed, the Great Sage Tarries

> *The myriad things have ever been one body;*
> *Each body, too, contains a cosmos.*
> *I dare open a clear eye on the world,*
> *And strive to root anew its hills and streams.*
> —An Old Rhyme

This chapter describes how the Ch'ing Fish confuses and bewitches the Mind-Monkey.[1] One sees throughout that the causes of all emotions are floating clouds and phantasms.

As the story goes, after the T'ang Priest and his three disciples left the Flaming Mountain, days turned into months, until they came again to the time of green spring. The T'ang Priest sighed, "We four have traveled day in and day out, never knowing when we'll see Sakyamuni. Wu-k'ung,[2] you've been over the road to the West several times, how much farther do we have to go? And how many more monsters will we meet?"

Monkey replied, "Don't worry, Master. If we disciples pool our strength, we needn't fear even a monster as big as heaven."

He had hardly finished speaking when all at once they spied before them a mountain road. Everywhere flowers old and newly fallen covered the ground like a tapestry. There, where tall bamboo leaned over the road stood a peony tree:

---

[1] Mind-Monkey is a metaphor for the incessant activity of the *hsin* (which refers to both mind and heart) and its tendency to turn its attention from one thought to another like a monkey leaping from branch to branch in a tree. The Ch'ing Fish, literally a mackerel, was chosen by the author to stand for the demon desire because of the pun between the Chinese name for this fish and the word for desire.

[2] I.e., Monkey.

The famous flowers no sooner bloom'd than form'd this tapestry;
Clusters of blossoms press together, competing with beauty strange.
Like finely tailor'd brilliant clouds they face the sun and smile,
Tenderly holding fragrant dew and bending with the breeze.
Clouds love these famed beauties and come to protect them;
Butterflies cling to their heavenly fragrance and tarry over leaving.
Were I to compare their color with the ladies in the Spring Palace,
Only Yang Kuei-fei coquettishly leaning, half-drunk, would do.[3]

—An Old Rhyme

Said Monkey, "Master, those peonies are so red!"

The T'ang priest responded, "No they're not."

"Master," said Monkey, "Your eyes must be scorched by the hot spring sun if you insist that peonies so red aren't red. Why not dismount and sit down while I send for the Bodhisattva Great King of Medicine to clear up your eyes. Don't force yourself to go on while your vision is blurred. If you take the wrong road, it will be no one else's fault."

The Priest snapped, "Rascal monkey! You're the one who's mixed up. It's backwards to say that my eyes are blurred."

Monkey said, "Master, if your eyes aren't blurred, why do you say the peonies aren't red?"

The Priest replied, "I never said the peonies aren't red. I only said that it's not the peonies that are red."

Monkey said, "If it's not the peonies that are red, Master, it must be the sunlight shining on them that makes them so red."

When the Priest heard Monkey suggest sunlight, he decided that his disciple's thinking was even farther off. "Stupid ape!" he scolded. "It's you who's red! You talk about peonies, then about sunlight—you certainly drag in trivialities!"

Monkey said, "You must be joking, Master. All the hair on my body is mottled yellow, my tiger-skin kilt is striped, my monk's robe is gray. Where do you see red on me?"

The Priest said, "I didn't mean that your body is red. I meant that your heart is red." Then he said, "Wu-k'ung, listen to this *gāthā* of mine." From his horse he recited:

The peonies aren't red;
It's the disciple's heart that's red.

---

[3] Yang Kuei-fei was the favorite consort of T'ang Hsüan-tsung (r. 712–755). The emperor's infatuation with her was a factor that contributed to the disastrous An Lu-shan rebellion that ended his reign.

When all the blossoms have fallen,
It's as if they hadn't yet bloomed.

He finished the *gāthā*, and rode on a hundred paces.[4] There before them several hundred lasses, each one rosy as a spring bud, suddenly appeared beneath the peony tree. They frolicked, picking flowers, weaving grass mats, carrying baby boys and girls, and showing off their loveliness. When they saw the monks coming from the east, they giggled, covering their mouths with their sleeves.

The Priest was troubled. He called to Wu-k'ung, "Let's go by way of some other less traveled route. I'm afraid that in this spring meadow so fresh and green these beautiful children will lead us straight into trouble and entanglements."

Monkey said, "Master, I've been meaning to say a few words to you, but I'm always afraid of offending you, so I haven't dared speak. All your life you've suffered from two great ills. One is using your mind too much, the other is literary Ch'an.[5] What I mean by using your mind too much is that you are always fretting over this and that. Literary Ch'an means reciting poems and discussing principles, bringing up your past to verify the present, and talking about scriptures and *gāthās*. Literary Ch'an has nothing to do with our real goal, and using the mind too much actually invites demons. Overcome these ills and you'll be well prepared to go to the West."

The Priest was displeased. Monkey insisted, "You're mistaken, Master. They are homebodies, we're monks. We share one road, but we have two kinds of hearts."

Hearing this, the T'ang Priest sharply urged his horse forward. But suddenly eight or nine children jumped out from the crowd and surrounded him—a wall of boys and girls. They stared at him, then began to jump up and down, shouting, "This little boy has grown up, but he still wears raggedy beggar-boy clothes!"

Being by nature a man who loved tranquillity, how could the Priest put up with these children? He tried to talk them nicely into leaving, but

---

[4] *Gāthā* is a type of Buddhist poetry composed of four lines of unspecified length. In this case, the first two lines are four characters long, and the second two are five characters long.

[5] Ch'an is the Meditation School of Chinese Buddhism (known also by its Japanese pronunciation, Zen), whose tenets place primary emphasis on direct apprehension of the true nature of existence and hold reliance on such verbal means as composing and reciting poems and discussing texts such as sūtras and their commentaries to be secondary or supplementary in the effort to attain that goal.

they would not go. He scolded them, yet still they would not go, and only kept up their taunts, "This boy has grown up, but he still wears beggar-boy clothes!"

The Priest could not think of anything to do, so he dismounted, took off his robe, hid it in his bundle, and sat down on the grass. The children would not leave him alone, and taunted again, "Give us this one-colored raggedy beggar's robe. If you don't, we'll go home and ask our mothers to make us patched robes of apple green, dark green, willow green, *pi-i* bird color,[6] evening-cloud, swallow gray, sauce-brown, sky-blue, peach-pink, jade, lotus stem, lotus-green, silver-green, fish-belly white, ink-wash, pebble-blue, reed-flower green, five-color weave, lichee, coral, duck's head green, color of the palindrome weave, and love-weave. Then we won't need your robe!"

The T'ang Priest closed his eyes and remained silent. Pigsy did not know what was bothering the Master and only wanted to play with the boys and girls. He jokingly called them his adopted children.

Monkey watching this became restless and upset. He took his iron cudgel from behind his ear[7] and brandished it, forcing the crowd back. The children, now frightened, ran away, stumbling over one another. But Monkey's temper did not abate. In a flash he overtook them, swung his cudgel, and struck. Those sweet snail-horn tufts and peachy cheeks passed into oblivion, becoming so many butterflies and will-o'-the-wisps.

When the crowd of beauties under the peonies saw Monkey beating the children to death, they quickly dropped their flower baskets and ran to the edge of a nearby stream. Picking up slabs of rock, they came forward to meet Monkey. But Monkey did not hesitate; he knocked them dead to the ground with one sweep of his cudgel.

It so happened that Monkey, although brave and belligerent, was, nevertheless, compassionate. As he placed the cudgel back behind his ear, tears unconsciously flowed from his eyes, and he said to himself contritely, "Great Heaven! Since I became a Buddhist, I've controlled my emotions and contained my anger. I've never wrongly killed a single man. Today I struck out in sudden anger and killed boys and girls who

---

[6] The *pi-i* is a fabulous bird that has only one wing and must therefore be always with its mate in order to fly. They are said to be quick-green and crimson.

[7] Monkey possesses the enchanted cudgel that was originally used by the sage-emperor Yü in controlling the Great Floods and fixing the depths of the various waterways. Monkey acquired it from the Dragon King of the Eastern Sea in chapter 3 of *Journey to the West* and used its powers of transmogrification to keep it small enough to be tucked behind his ear or to be enlarged or multiplied as needed for battle.

weren't even monsters or thieves—old and young, maybe fifty in all. I completely forgot the heavy price for doing wrong."

Monkey took two steps, and was again overcome by fear. He said to himself, "I've been thinking only of hell in the future. I'd completely forgotten the hell that is right in front of me. The day before yesterday I killed a monster, and right away the Master wanted to chant the charm.[8] Once when I killed several thieves, the Master renounced me on the spot. When he sees this pile of corpses today, he'll really be angry. If he chants the charm a hundred times, this noble Great Sage Sun[9] will be one skinned monkey. Will I have any honor left then?"

But after all, Mind-Monkey was intelligent and resourceful. He came up with another idea. He knew our old monk was a man of culture, but he was also overly compassionate, and the bones in his ears were soft.[10] To himself he said, "Today I'll write a eulogy for these wrongly killed innocents. I'll put on a crying face and read it as I walk. When the Master sees me crying so, he'll surely be suspicious and say, 'Wu-k'ung, what's happened to that old pluck of yours?' I'll say, 'There are monsters on the Western road.' The Master's suspicion will increase. He'll ask, 'Where are these monsters? What are they called?' I'll say, 'They're called "man-beating monsters." If you don't believe me, take a look and you'll see that the crowd of boys and girls have become bloody corpses.' When Master hears how terrible the monsters are, his courage will fail and his heart will leap. Pigsy will say, 'Let's get out of here.' Sandy will say, 'Let's go, fast!' When I see that they're well shaken, I'll comfort them with one word: 'Everything's been taken care of by Kuan-yin. There's not one tile left unbroken in the monster's cave!'"

Monkey straightaway found a rock to use for an ink-stone and broke a plum branch for a brush. He ground mud into ink and stripped bamboo to make paper. Then he wrote out the eulogy. Gathering up his sleeves like a scholar, he swaggered with long strides and loudly recited:

> I, Monkey, first disciple of the Great Buddhist Master Hsüan-tsang, who received from the legitimate Emperor of the Great T'ang a hundred-pearled cassock, a five-pearled abbot's staff, and the title 'Brother of the Emperor,'

---

[8] The charm in question is an incantation that causes Monkey's gold-inlaid flowered cap to constrict, causing him unbearable pain. The magic cap was given to the T'ang Priest by Bodhisattva Kuan-yin in chapter 14 of *Journey to the West* as a check on Monkey's volatile temper.

[9] Monkey's surname is Sun.

[10] Having soft bones in the ears means that one is not able to resist sweet words, pleas or lies.

as the Master of Water-curtain Cave, Great Sage Equal of Heaven, Rebel in the Heavenly Palace, and Eminent Guest in the Underworld, Sun Wu-k'ung, do reverently offer as sacrifice clear wine and simple food and write this message to you, spirits of the boys and girls in the spring wind, against whom I bore no grudge and harbored no enmity:

Alas! The willows by the gate have turned to gold; orchids in the courtyard are pregnant with jade. Heaven and Earth are unkind; the green-in-years reach no fruition. Oh, why do their waistbands drift among peach blossoms this third month on the River Hsiang? Why do the white crane's clouds twine with the endless mist to the Ninth Heaven? Ah, Ye spirits, how can I send you off? I bear a secret sorrow for you.

And furthermore, where dragons and snakes are coiled around bronze columns, in the great hall busy with silkworms, with her jade lute weeping for the wind and rain, in the tower, crying like a tiger—such was the decorum of the White Girl. Oh, why, when spring clothes are ready and spring grasses green, and when spring days grow longer, are spring lives cut short? Ah, Ye spirits! How can I send you off? I bear a secret sorrow for you.

Alas! A hobbyhorse ride of a mile, a firefly bag half-filled—Little Boy Fate had no call for anger. The money for washing has not been given, but little bird shoes have flown to the Western Abyss; a pair of pillars, first decked in red, now don white goosefeather robes and play in the Purple Vale. Ah, Ye spirits! How can I send you off? I bear a secret sorrow for you.

And think of Confucius, who, as a lad of seven hid in the bed curtains and chirped like a cricket! And think of Tseng Shen, who when only two feet tall offered lichees from under the stairs! Oh why do you no longer speak of such proprieties? Jade is split in the southern field, a lotus shatters on the eastern lake. The jujubes, floating red, are not gathered; the sap that hangs from the *t'ung* tree is not chewed. Ah, Ye spirits! How can I send you off? I bear a secret sorrow for you.

Alas! Not to the South or North or West or East can I write lines to bring back your souls. Are you Chang or Ch'ien or Hsü or Chao? How can I tell from these old gravestones? Ah, Ye spirits! How can I send you off? I bear a secret sorrow for you.[11]

By the time Monkey finished reading, he had come to the peony tree. He saw the Master asleep, his head drooped on his chest, while Sandy and Pigsy lay sleeping with their heads on a stone. Monkey laughed to himself, "The old monk is usually more vigorous—he's never been so drowsy. My stars are lucky today! I won't have to suffer from the charm."

---

[11] This seems to be Monkey's attempt at "literary Ch'an." Clearly, its opaqueness and ineptness is meant to satirize this kind of practice.

Then he picked some grass and flowers, and after rolling them into a ball, stuffed them in Pigsy's ear. He yelled in the other ear, "Wu-neng![12] Don't have upside-down dreams!"

Pigsy mumbled a reply in his dream, "Master, why are you calling me?"

Monkey realized that in his dream Pigsy mistook him for the Master, so he imitated the Master's voice and said, "Disciple, Bodhisattva Kuan-yin passed here and asked me to give you her regards."

With his eyes closed Pigsy mumbled through the grass, "Has the Bodhisattva said anything behind my back?"

Monkey said, "Oh my, yes! The Bodhisattva just now evaluated me and you three as well. First she said that I couldn't become a buddha and told me not to go to the Western Paradise. She said Wu-k'ung will surely become a buddha, and that he should go on to the Western Paradise alone. Wu-ching[13] can be a monk. She said he should go and cultivate himself in a pure temple along the Western road. After making these three comments, the Bodhisattva stared at you and said, 'Wu-neng likes his sleep. He'll never reach the Western Paradise either. Please tell him that I said he should take a loving and faithful wife.'"

Pigsy said, "I don't want the Western Paradise or a lovely wife! I just want half a day in the dark sweet village of sleep." And he snored like a bull.

When Monkey saw that he wouldn't wake up, he laughed and said, "Disciple, I'll go on ahead." Then he went west to beg for food.

---

[12] I.e., Pigsy.
[13] I.e., Sandy.

CHAPTER TWO

A New T'ang Dynasty Appears on the Western Road;
The Glorious Emperor Rests in the Green Jade Palace.

From here on, Wu-k'ung devises a thousand schemes to fool others, but instead only fools himself.

Monkey leaped onto his magic cloud and looked east and west for a place to beg for food. Two hours later he had yet to see a single house and was growing impatient. Just as he was about to lower his cloud and return to the old road, he spied a great city surrounded by a moat ten miles off. He hurried in to take a look, and saw that on the city wall flew a green embroidered banner. In golden seal-style characters the banner announced: "Great T'ang's New Son-of-Heaven, the Restoration Emperor, Thirty-eighth Successor of T'ai-tsung."[1]

When Monkey spotted the two words "Great T'ang," he gave a start and broke out in a cold sweat. He thought, "We've been traveling west; how could we have returned to the east? This can't be real. I wonder what monster is doing evil here." Then he had another thought, "I've heard the earth is round and the sky goes around it. Perhaps we passed the Western Paradise and have come around again. If that's so, we shouldn't worry—we'll just have to go around once more, and we'll reach the Western Paradise. Maybe this is real after all."

But after reconsideration he rejected that idea, "It's not real. No! If we passed the Western Paradise, why didn't the Compassionate Buddha call out to me? After all, I've seen him several times, and he's not an unfeeling or inhospitable person. This has got to be a hoax."

Then he recalled, "When I was a demon at Water-curtain Cave,[2] I had a sworn brother who called himself Messenger-in-Blue. He gave me

---

[1] *Journey to the West* is set in the reign of the second emperor of the T'ang dynasty, T'ai-tsung (r. 627–649).

[2] At the opening of *Journey to the West* Monkey ruled as the king of the monkey inhabitants of Water-curtain Cave in the Mountain of Flowers and Fruit.

a book entitled *Apocryphal History of the K'un-lun Mountains*. In one place it said, 'There was a kingdom called China that wasn't originally called China. Its people envied the name China and consequently adopted it.' This kingdom must be the place in the West that took the name 'China.' So it is real."

An instant later Monkey blurted out, "False! False! False! False! False! If they were envious of China, they would only have written 'China.' Why did they write 'Great T'ang?' What's more, my Master often says that the Great T'ang is quite a new empire. How could they already know the name here and change their banner? It can't be real."

After a long time he still hadn't made up his mind, so he decided to take a closer look and read the rest of the banner. When he read

> "New Son of Heaven, the Restoration Emperor, Thirty-eighth Successor of T'ai-tsung,"

he stamped his feet and shouted into the sky, "Nonsense! Nonsense! It hasn't been twenty years since the Master left the realm of the Great T'ang. How could a dynasty already have passed several hundred years? The Master is only flesh and blood. Even though he's been in and out of the caves of spirits and immortals and visited fairy islands, he still passes his days like any ordinary man. How could there be such a difference? It has to be false."

But he considered again, "You can't tell—if they changed emperors each month, they could go through thirty-eight emperors in less than four years. Maybe it is real."

The fog of doubt had not been dispersed, and all this reasoning was getting him nowhere. So he lowered his cloud and chanted an incantation to summon the local deity for information. He repeated it ten times, but no deity came. Monkey thought, "Usually when I recite just a little of it, they shield their heads and come running like rats. What's going on today? Well, this is for something urgent, so I won't punish him. I'll call the celestial officials on duty today. They'll know the answer for sure."

Trying to locate the celestial officials, he shouted toward the sky several hundred times, but couldn't find a trace of them. Monkey was furious. In a twinkling he changed into the form in which he had caused an uproar in Heaven,[3] and brandished his cudgel till it was as big around

---

[3] In chapter 7 of *Journey to the West* Monkey goes on a rampage in the Heavenly Palace of the Jade Emperor until he is finally subdued by Buddha.

as the mouth of a barrel. He sprang into the air, jumping and whirling wildly. He carried on for a long while, but not so much as a lowly deity answered him.

Monkey became even angrier. He rushed headlong to the Palace of Magic Mists to see the Jade Emperor and demand an explanation from him. But when he got there he found the gates of Heaven tightly closed.

Monkey yelled, "Open the door! Open the door!"

Someone inside replied, "Listen to this impetuous slave, will you? Someone has stolen our Palace of Magic Mists. There's no Heaven to be entered."

He heard someone else laugh and say, "Didn't you know our Palace was stolen, big brother? Five hundred years ago there was a Stable Master Sun[4] who caused an uproar in Heaven. He didn't manage to steal the Palace of Magic Mists, but he carried a grudge and formed a gang, and while pretending he was going to get scriptures, he made friends with all the monsters on the Western road. Then one day he summoned those monsters and used several ingenious devices to steal the Palace. That's what's called in military strategy 'Using others to attack others—an infallible plan.' That ape is really a schemer! He's quite something!"

When Monkey heard this, he was both amused and annoyed. But being a stubborn and impatient fellow, how could he swallow these false charges? He beat on the gate again with his fists and kicked it, shouting "Open the door!"

The voice inside spoke again. "If you really want to open the gates of Heaven, wait five thousand and forty-six years until the new Palace of Magic Mists is completed. Then we'll open the gates to receive you, honored guest. How's that?"

Monkey had hoped to see the Jade Emperor and get a divinely worded scroll in purple characters that would state clearly whether the Great T'ang he had seen was true or false. Instead he had been greatly humiliated. He could do nothing but lower his cloud and return to the domain of the Great T'ang, saying, "I'll just go on in and see what happens."

Thereupon he forgot his annoyance and walked through the city gate. The guard at the gate said, "The new Emperor has ordered that anyone who speaks or dresses strangely is to be seized and killed. You, little monk, with no home or family, should watch out for yourself."

---

[4] Prior to his rebellion in Heaven, Monkey held the position of Stable Master of the Heavenly Palace.

Monkey saluted with his clasped hands and said "Your words, Sir, are most considerate." He hurried through the gate, then changed himself into a black and white butterfly and flew along like the dance of a beautiful girl or the notes of a lute.

Soon he reached the base of a colorful tower. He fluttered through its jade gate and came to rest in a hall. The jade hinges of the many doors were wound around with mist; the green chambers were wrapped in clouds. Even fairies never see such sights—an immortal's cave hardly compares.

The heavens revolve, the golden breath unites;
The stars move until the Dipper's handle becomes level.
A cloud forms in the Kingfisher Palace;
The sun shines bright in Phoenix City.
　　　　　　　　　—An Old Rhyme

Monkey looked and looked. He noticed on the door-lintel of the hall three large characters which read, "Green Jade Palace." Beside this was inscribed a line of small characters: "This palace was built on an auspicious day in the second month of the first year of the Romantic Emperor of the New T'ang." The hall was silent, but on one wall were two lines of calligraphy: "When the T'ang dynasty had held the mandate less than fifty years, that great country was reduced to the size of a peck. Fifty years after the T'ang received the mandate, the mountains and streams flew about, the stars and the moon left their courses. But the new emperor has held the mandate for a hundred million years. People everywhere sing the odes written for King Hsüan of Chou.[5] I, the minor official Chang Ch'iu, reverently offer praise."

When Monkey read this, he laughed to himself and said: "With insignificant officials like this at court, how could the emperor help but be romantic?"

At that moment an imperial concubine entered carrying a green bamboo broom. She chuckled to herself, "Oh-ho! The emperor is asleep, the prime minister is, too. This Green Jade Palace is now a "Sleeping Immortal Pavilion." Last night our Romantic Emperor warmed the room of Lady Ch'ing-kuo.[6] He ordered wine taken to Flying Kingfisher

---

[5] The Chinese original is obscure here. The author probably compares the New T'ang Emperor to King Hsüan of Chou (r. 827–780 B.C.), who brought about a restoration of the Chou dynasty.

[6] Lady Ch'ing-kuo (Ch'ing-kuo fu-jen) literally means "lady whose beauty can topple a state."

Palace for a merry night of drinking. Early in the evening he brought out a Kao-t'ang mirror[7] and told Lady Ch'ing-kuo to stand on his left and Lady Hsü to stand on his right. As they stood three abreast gazing into the mirror, the emperor said, 'You two ladies are lovely!' Lady Ch'ing-kuo said, 'Your Majesty is handsome.' The emperor turned his head to ask the opinion of us concubines, and all three hundred of us who are intimate with him replied together, 'Your Majesty is indeed the world's finest.'

"The emperor was delighted. He narrowed his eyes and tossed off a great horn of wine. When he was half-drunk he got up to look at the moon, then opened his mouth and laughed. Pointing at Ch'ang O[8] in the moon, he said, 'That's my Lady Hsü.' Lady Hsü pointed at the stars of the Spinning Lady and the Cowherd and said, 'There are Your Majesty and Lady Ch'ing-kuo. Although tonight is only the fifth of the third month, you have in advance the evening of the seventh month.'[9] The emperor was greatly pleased and again drank his great horn empty.

"A drunken emperor—face flushed, head nodding, legs staggering, tongue thick; oblivious to the fact that three sevens are twenty-one and two sevens are fourteen—toppled across Lady Hsü's body. Lady Ch'ing-kuo quickly sat down and folded herself into a snowflake mat of flesh to pillow the emperor's heels. At Lady Hsü's side sat a young maid of rather good taste who straightaway plucked a fragrant seatree flower. Giggling, she walked behind Lady Hsü and lightly placed it on the emperor's head, making him a drunken Flower Emperor. Such a happy time! It was really a fairy island on earth.

"Still, when you think of it, past generations had many emperors, and not a few romantic ones. Today their palaces are gone, the lovely ladies are gone, the emperors, all gone. There's really no need to mention Ch'in and Han and the Six Dynasties—even our late emperor in his middle age loved to seek pleasure. He built Pearl-rain Tower—so

---

[7] Kao-t'ang is the name of a terrace in the Yün-meng Marshes in the ancient state of Ch'u. According to legend, King Hsiang of Ch'u once visited the terrace and dreamed that he slept with the Goddess of Wu Mountain. In Chinese literature, therefore, allusions to Kao-t'ang always have erotic connotations.

[8] Ch'ang O is a mythical lady supposed to live in the moon. She was originally the wife of the archer Hou I during the reign of the sage-emperor Yao. Ch'ang O stole some elixir from her husband and, after having taken it, flew to the moon, where she still lives in eternal loneliness.

[9] Spinning Lady and the Cowherd are a pair of lovers associated in folklore with the stars Vega and Altair. Separated by the Milky Way, they are fated to meet only once each year, on the seventh of the seventh moon.

elegant! It was trellised with white jade, and on all four sides carved green ornaments hung from the windows. On the north stood a round frost-cave gate where you could watch the sun rise and set in the sea. The stairs below were made of red sandalwood edged with gold. Painted lotus-faces, powdered plum-petal skin, cicada-wing blouses and unicorn belts, flutes of Shu and strings of Wu[10]—no one saw all this without envy or heard all this without being moved.

"Yesterday the empress told me to go and sweep the grounds of the eastern flower garden. I looked over the short wall to see Pearl-rain Tower, and at first I saw only desolate grass. I looked again. There were clouds and mist, and what had been three thousand interlocking tiles were a million fragments. Beams carved with whirling dragons and timbers carved with flying insects stood like broken trellises.

"But there was something still more absurd. The sun was only half-way up the sky, but several will-o'-the-wisps came from the well by the pines. When I looked closely, there wasn't a single singing-boy or dancing-girl in sight, only two or three cuckoos calling over and over—one high note and one low note in the spring rain.

"When you see this sort of thing, you realize that emperor and commoner all return to nothing; imperial concubine and village girl alike become dust. Last year on the fifteenth of the first month, the Taoist Sung Lo spoke a bit of wisdom. He said, 'Our Romantic Emperor enjoys seeing people in paintings and loves the scenery in pictures.' So he presented a painting called 'A Portrait of Mt. Li.' The emperor asked, 'Is Mt. Li still in existence?' The Taoist said, 'Mt. Li has had a short life of only two thousand years.' The emperor laughed and said, 'Two thousand years is enough.' The Taoist said, 'I only regret that it has not been two thousand years in a row. The Mt. Li of earth and wood lasted only two hundred years; people talked about it for four hundred years; it's been depicted in writings, calligraphic works, and paintings for five hundred years, and recorded in history for nine hundred years. Adding up these fragments you get two thousand years.'

"That day I was in attendance, standing right in front of the Taoist. I heard every sentence clearly. That was over a year ago, and just the day before yesterday, I visited a learned imperial concubine and spoke to her of this. She told me that the 'Portrait of Mt. Li' really showed the grave

---

[10] Shu is the classical name for the area of present-day Szechwan province, and Wu is the classical name for the area of present-day Kiangsu and Chekiang Provinces.

of the First August Emperor of Ch'in, who once used the Mountain-removing Bell."[11]

The girl swept and talked and talked and swept.

When Monkey heard the words, "Mountain-removing Bell," he thought, "How can a mountain be removed? . . . Why, if I had that bell, whenever I came to a high mountain where monsters lived, I could just remove it in advance and save myself trouble." He was about to change himself into a court attendant and go ask the concubine more about the magical bell, when suddenly he heard loud strains of flute and drum music coming from the main palace.

---

[11] The First Emperor of Ch'in was the ruler who effected the unification of China in 221 B.C. and was the first to assume the imperial title.

CHAPTER THREE

Hsüan-tsang Is To Be Commissioned and Given a Peach Flower Battle-Axe; The Mind-Monkey Is Startled by the Axes of Sky Gougers.

When Monkey heard the music he flew right out through Tiger Gate. After passing many towers and courtyards, he finally came to a carved green portico where the emperor sat surrounded by numerous officials. As he drew near, he saw the emperor blanch and say to his officials: "Yesterday I was reading the *Precious Instructions of the August T'ang*. One section related, 'The T'ang priest Ch'en Hsüan-tsang impersonated a monk and deluded our royal ancestor. His disciples were all Water-curtain Cave and Stony Brook[1] types. Abbot's staff and begging bowl became weapons like the wooden rake[2] and metal cudgel. Forty years later, Hsüan-tsang led his disciples on an invasion of our territory. He was indeed a great enemy.'

"Another section related that 'five hundred years ago Sun Wu-k'ung rebelled against Heaven. He wanted to drag the Jade Emperor down from his throne and deposit him at the bottom of the stairs. However, the Mandate of Heaven had not expired, and Buddha put down the rebellion. If Sun Wu-K'ung could rebel against Heaven, how much more could he rebel against mortals? And yet the T'ang Priest accepted him as his number-one disciple. Why? He wanted to use his journey to the West to establish hegemony over the Southeast. He relied on the awesomeness of the ape and his dragon-horse[3] to secure his position as a shark among fish.'

"When I read those words, I became frightened. But if I order Regional Commander Chao Ch'eng to go west to decapitate this priest

---

[1] Stony Brook was Sandy's original haunt.
[2] The wooden rake is the weapon wielded by Pigsy.
[3] The dragon-horse is the T'ang Priest's mount—a dragon transformed into a horse by Kuan-yin.

31

and bring back his head, then spare his disciples and cause them to disperse, that should put an end to the matter."

The Vice Director of State Affairs Li K'uang stepped forward and said, "This bald-headed Ch'en Hsüan-tsang shouldn't be killed—he should be used. You should simply use him to kill himself; you shouldn't have someone else kill him."

As soon as Li K'uang finished speaking the emperor ordered his generals to go to the arsenal. There they selected a flying dragon sword, a King Wu blade, a stone sickle, a thunder-flower lance, an ornately carved five-cloud spear, a black-horse breastplate, silver-fish armor, a flying-tiger jade tent-standard, a great Yao and Shun banner, a peach blossom battle-axe, a ninth-month axe, a glass moon-mirror helmet, a red and gold flying-fish cape, a pair of demon-killing crystal-threaded boots, and a Big Dipper fan. All these things were sealed along with an imperial edict on yellow silk and sent by express messenger to the West. The proclamation, addressed to "Ch'en Hsüan-tsang, Brother of the Emperor, Supreme Commander for Wiping out Desire," read:

O great and trustworthy General, honorable as the tallies of jadeite, straight as the red strings of a lute: Yesterday all the lords from every direction spurred their horses to the Fatherland and competed with each other to report your martial valor, which has left the mermaids of the western region speechless and the mirages at sea without form. It is difficult to find a man such as you in time of crisis or prosperity. We have often admired you and have heard only good about you. We turn our eyes to the western mountains and sigh with grief. Now bandits run amok in the West. Reports come daily from the passes. This is because Heaven resents separations, and it is time that you, Our mendicant monk, return. General, why don't you leap up from your white pool and beat your sword of intelligence, take off your dark robe and pour out your bag of wisdom? After you've cleared the green wood of bandits and the beacon fires no longer burn, We will personally bind the head of your horse with one foot of white silk. This day you will carry a carved spear and wear silver armor. Soon you will sleep in tents painted with beasts. It would be difficult to inscribe Our expressions of tearful thanks for your deeds, even on all the pillars of the K'un-lun Mountains that support Heaven. Who under the sun that hangs on Heaven's Wall could compose fitting words upon your return? We hope you, General, will mull this over once and then again. We have long wearied of resorting to coral bow and green-jade arrows.

The emperor ordered a jade tally brought from the palace and gave it to a messenger. Having received the imperial order, the messenger took the tally, the seal, and the edict and galloped out of the city.

Monkey was shocked and afraid something might happen to entangle his Master. Not daring to make a sound, he immediately started in pursuit of the messenger. He fluttered down like a plum blossom, landing outside the city gate. There he resumed his normal appearance and searched for the messenger, but the messenger had already ridden out of sight. Monkey became even more distressed. Not only had he failed to discover the truth or falsehood of the New T'ang, now he had heard that, out of the blue, his Master was to be made a general. Monkey was startled, frightened, and seized with melancholy. As he jumped up to go search for his Master, he heard voices high in the air. He peered up and saw a great crowd of people swinging axes and using chisels to gouge holes in the sky.

Monkey considered, "They don't have the look of celestial workers or ominous or evil stars. They are obviously people from earth, but why are they doing this sort of work there? They aren't monsters disguised as men because I see no evil aura about them. Could it be that Heaven is infected with scabies and needs people to scratch its back? Or maybe Heaven has grown extra bones and has asked a surgeon to remove them? Or maybe Heaven is too old and they are chiseling it away so they can put in a new one. Or maybe Heaven has been covered by a screen, and they are removing the false Heaven for the real one. Or maybe the Milky Way has flooded and they are channeling away the excess. Or maybe they are rebuilding the Palace of Magic Mists and this is an auspicious day to break ground. Or maybe Heaven likes elaboration and has asked these people to carve a myriad lines to make a beautiful scene. Or maybe the Jade Emperor misses this mortal world and they are opening an imperial road so he can visit more often.

"I wonder if Heaven's blood is red or white. Or if Heaven's skin is one or two layers thick. Or if there will be a heart or not when Heaven's chest is opened. Or if Heaven's heart is slanted or straight. Or if Heaven is young or old, if it's male or female. Maybe they want to open Heaven and let its mountains hang down and dwarf the earth's mountains. Or maybe they are opening a mouth for Heaven to swallow the Underworld. But even if any of these things are true, no one on earth could have such power. I'll just go up and ask them; then I'll know for sure."

Monkey shouted, "You officers digging at Heaven! What king's men are you? Why are you doing this strange thing?"

All of them dropped their axes and chisels and saluted Monkey from the sky. They said, "Your Reverence from the Southeast, we are called Sky-walkers and come from Goldfish Village. Twenty years ago a wandering Taoist taught us the method of sky walking. In our village everyone knows how to write and recite charms and ride the clouds, so we changed the name of the village from Goldfish to Sky-walking Village. All our children are called Sky-walkers. Everyone in our village can move about in the sky.

"Who would have thought that when the king of the Emerald Green World—who is called Little Moon King—recently took in a monk, that the monk would turn out to be the second master of Sun Wu-k'ung, the Eminent Guest of the Underworld, Rebel in Heaven, Great Sage Equal of Heaven, and Master of Water-curtain Cave? He was none other than the great T'ang priest Hsüan-tsang, who received from the legitimate emperor of the Great T'ang a cassock studded with a hundred jewels, a five-colored abbot's staff, and the title 'Emperor's Younger Brother.'

"This priest, whose secular name is Ch'en, was pure and chaste, never eating meat or drinking wine, nor allowing his eye to roam. He was more than qualified to go to the Western Paradise. But that Monkey Sun was berserk! He cut people down as if they were grass. The road to the West flowed red with the blood of his victims. When people talk about him they grind their teeth in hatred.

"The ruler of the kingdom called Great Compassion has taken pity on the suffering people and completely blocked the road to the West with a bronze wall that reaches to the sky. Knowing that Monkey could transform himself and become tall or short, he spread a closely meshed 'net of longing' for sixty thousand miles to go with the bronze wall. Since then, the western and eastern heavens have been divided in two. There is no way to cross over—not by boat or cart, water or land. On learning this, the T'ang Priest was utterly crushed. That Monkey just stamped his feet and ran off. The priest's second disciple, Pigsy, and third disciple, Sandy, could only cry, and the white horse the priest rides wouldn't eat even a mouthful of grass.

"In this moment of crisis, the T'ang Priest came up with a plan. He told his second and third disciples not to worry, whipped his horse and galloped into the Emerald Green World. The moment Little Moon King saw the priest, he was sure they had been lovers in a previous life and treated him like his own flesh and blood. He insisted on giving his Emerald Green World to the priest, but the T'ang Priest firmly refused, being determined only to go to the Western Paradise. Then Little Moon

King tried to press against the priest, and the Tang Priest had to push him off.

The king kept making advances but the monk just kept pushing him away.

"After several days, Little Moon King had thought of nothing that might solve the Priest's problem, so he summoned the worthies of the realm for consultation. One of them devised a plan: 'If you could find some sky gougers, they could open up Heaven and allow Mr. Ch'en to leap right into the Jade Emperor's palace. There he could ask for a pass and proceed directly to the Western Paradise. That seems like a good idea.'

"Little Moon King was half pleased and half doubtful, but he straightaway called out soldiers and cavalry to search everywhere for sky gougers. When they came across a group of us catching wild geese in the air, they moved in on us. One general in golden armor waved his arms, pointed at us excitedly, and shouted, 'Here are the sky gougers! Surround them for me, little soldiers. Get them all, every one. Put them in cangues and chains and we'll take them to the king.'

"Little Moon King was delighted. He ordered his men to remove the cangues and take off the chains and immediately had fine red wine brought and given to us. Then he forced us to chip away at the sky. As the saying goes, 'The skilful don't seem busy, and the busy aren't skilful.' We do all sorts of other things, but we aren't used to digging into the sky with axes. Today we were treated so nicely by the king that we had no choice but to sharpen our tools and force ourselves to learn to dig at the firmament. We've been looking up for so long that our necks are stiff, and standing in the air so long that our legs ache. Around noon we pooled our strength and with one thrust cracked into Heaven.

How were we to know we hit right at the foundation of the Palace of Magic Mists and caused it, all shiny and bright, to come tumbling down? There was a great commotion in Heaven and people yelled, 'Catch the thieves!' The panic didn't ease up for a long time.

"But the stars must be with us, because someone else will take the blame for what we did. After the commotion died down we were pretty scared. But when we bent our ears to listen, we heard Lao-tzu tell the Jade Emperor, 'Don't be angry. Don't get upset. This couldn't be the work of anyone but that little slave-dog of a Stable Groom, Monkey Sun. If you send out Heavenly soldiers now, I'm afraid there'll be trouble. It would be better to ask Buddha to crush him beneath Five Phases Mountain. We must tell Buddha that Monkey is never again to be set free.'

"When we heard this, we knew we were in the clear, or at least we figured someone would take the blame, so we began to dig here again. There won't be another Palace of Magic Mists to tumble down.

But it's too bad about Monkey Sun. In the world below he's hated all along the road to the West, and in the world above they rage at him. They've also sent word to Buddha, and when Kuan-yin sees that Buddha puts the blame on the ape, she won't dare welcome him with her usual graces. Then we'll see where he can go!"

Someone else said, "Bah! Why feel sorry for that ape Sun? If it weren't for that slave-dog ape, we wouldn't be working here."

All the people wielding axes cried, "You're right! Curse that ape!" A great roar went up, with everyone shouting different things at the same time. "Stable Boy!" "Wine Thief!"[4] "Elixir Stealer!" "Ginseng Robber!" "Monkey Monster Tramp!" They cursed Monkey till his golden eyes blurred and his copper bones went numb.

---

[4] The rebukes of Wine Thief, Elixir Stealer, and Ginseng Robber allude to several of Monkey's escapades earlier in *Journey to the West*.

CHAPTER FOUR

A Crack Reveals a Myriad of Bewildering Mirrors;
Where the Shapes of Things Appear, Their Original Form Is Lost.

Subjected to these groundless accusations and cursed in such a humiliating way, Monkey became furious. He wanted to go up and kill them all but he thought, "When I left him, the Master was peacefully resting on the grass. What's he doing here in the Emerald Green World? This Little Moon King must be a demon."

Dear Monkey didn't waste any words, but left in a bound. Coming around a turn, he was confronted by a city wall with a moat. Above the city gate hung a flecked moss-green jade placard with three words inscribed in the seal style: "Emerald Green World." The two halves of the gate were ajar, and Monkey, quite pleased, walked briskly in. Inside the gate, however, he ran into another sheer wall towering before him. He ran along its entire length and back again, but he couldn't find a single crack through which he might pass.

Monkey laughed and said, "What kind of city is this? Could it be that there isn't a single person here? But if there weren't people, why would a wall have been built? Let me take a closer look."

He searched for a long time, but there was indeed no way through. Again his anger mounted. He pounded to the east and pounded to the west, pounded high and low—pounded until he knocked down a piece of green stone.

Monkey tripped on the stone and fell into a brilliant place.

Recovering, he blinked and looked about. He was in a tower made entirely of costly stones. Above, a great sheet of agate formed the roof, and the floor was a huge bright slab. A couch of amethyst, ten chairs of green marble, and a glistening pink table, on which stood an onyx teapot and two turquoise bells, furnished the place. Facing him were eight sapphire blue windows, all closed.

Monkey could not see where he had come in and felt bewildered. He looked up and saw that the four walls were made of precious mirrors placed one above another. In all there must have been a million mirrors—large, small, and odd-shaped; square ones, round ones, and others. He couldn't count them all, but a few of the ones he recognized included a Heavenly Emperor mirror with an animal-shaped hook; a white jade heart mirror; a self-doubt mirror; a blossom mirror; a wind mirror; a pair of bird mirrors, male and female; a mirror that looked like a purple cotton lotus; a water mirror; an ice-terrace mirror; an iron-faced lotus mirror; a "me" mirror; a man mirror; a moon mirror; a Hai-nan mirror; a mirror in the shape of Emperor Wu of Han[1] pining for his lady; a green lock mirror; a stillness mirror; a nothing mirror; a bronze mirror with seal-style characters in the hand of Li Ssu of the Ch'in dynasty; a parrot mirror; a mute mirror; a mirror that retains reflections; a mirror shaped like the first concubine of Emperor Hsüan-yüan;[2] a one-smile mirror; a pillow mirror; a reflectionless mirror; and a flying mirror.

Monkey thought, "This will be fun. Let me reflect a hundred, a thousand, ten thousand, and a hundred million of me." He went to start mirroring himself, but instead of his own image, what he saw was that every mirror contained other heavens and earths, suns and moons, mountains and forests.

Amazed, he could do nothing but let his eyes wander. All at once he heard someone calling in a loud voice, "Reverend Sun, how have you been these many years since we parted?"

Monkey looked all around, but there was no one, and no ghostly aura in the tower. But the voice he heard couldn't have come from anywhere else. Thoroughly confused, he suddenly spied a man holding a steel trident and standing by the inside face of a square mirror with an animal-shaped hook. Again he called loudly, "Reverend Sun, you needn't look surprised. I'm an old friend."

Monkey moved closer. "You do look familiar," he said, "but I can't place you."

---

[1] Emperor Wu of the Han dynasty reigned from 141 to 87 B.C.

[2] Hsüan-yüan was the personal name of the Yellow Emperor, one of the five ancient mythical sage-emperors in China.

The figure responded, "My name is Liu Po-ch'in. When you came out from under Five Phases Mountain I lent you a hand.[3] But you've forgotten so soon! That's how it is with people's feelings."

Monkey quickly bowed most politely and said, "Ten thousand pardons, great benefactor. What are you doing now? How is it that we're here in the same place?"

Po-ch'in said, "Why do you say 'in the same place?' You're in somebody else's world and I'm in your world. It's not the same place at all!"

Monkey said, "Since it's not the same, how can we see each other?"

Po-ch'in said, "No, no, you don't understand. Little Moon King built this tower of myriad mirrors. Every mirror takes care of one world; and each blade of grass, each tree, everything moving and still, is contained in these mirrors. Anything one might want to see comes before one's eyes. So this tower was named 'The Three-thousand Major Chiliocosms!'"[4]

Monkey had another thought. He was about to ask something about the T'ang emperor in order to decide whether the New T'ang was real, when suddenly he saw an old lady dart out from the dark forest and push Liu Po-ch'in head over heels into the woods. They didn't come out again.

Monkey was disappointed and stepped back. Seeing that the daylight had already faded to evening he mused, "It will soon be dark and I haven't found the Master. I might as well take a good look into these mirrors. Then I'll decide what to do."

So he began at the first of the mirrors that hung beneath the word "Heaven." He saw there a man posting the results of the civil service examination. On the placard was written:

PALACE EXAMINATION
for
The Cultivated Talent Degree

FIRST PLACE	LIU CH'UN
SECOND PLACE	WU YU
THIRD PLACE	KAO WEI-MING

---

[3] In chapter 14 of *Journey to the West* Liu Po-ch'in accompanied the T'ang Priest to Five Phases Mountain, where the Priest secured Monkey's release from the Buddha's spell, which held him prisoner.

[4] Chiliocosm is a Buddhist concept of the universe. A small chiliocosm consists of a thousand worlds each with its Mt. Sumeru, continents, seas, and ring of iron mountains. A major chiliocosm consists of three thousand great chiliocosms.

Soon a crowd of thousands had gathered, shouting and excited to read the placard. At first, Monkey could make out only a general clamor, but then came sounds of crying and cursing. Finally the crowd broke up and people walked away one by one. Monkey watched as one of them sat vacantly on a stone; one smashed his inkstand; one with his hair hanging like wilted weeds was being chased and swatted by his parents and teachers; one opened the case he clutched to his side, took out his jade lute, burned it, then cried bitterly; one who took a sword from the headboard of his bed and tried to kill himself was stopped by a girl; one, his head bowed absentmindedly, took out his own essay and read it over and over; one laughed loudly and pounded the table shouting "It's damned fate!"; one hung his head and vomited blood; several elders bought spring wine to help ease the depression of another; one chanting poems alone wildly kicked a stone at the end of each line of verse; one wouldn't allow his boyservants to report that his name had not appeared on the list; one seemed angry and depressed but smiled frostily to himself as if to say, "I got what I deserved"; one was truly angry and unhappy but forced a smile.

Of the group whose names appeared on the list, one of them put on new clothes and shoes; one forced himself not to smile; one wrote on a wall; one read his own examination paper a thousand times, then carefully put it in his sleeve and went out; one sighed in sympathy for the others; one made a point of saying that the examining officials were not up to par; one made some companions read the placard, and, though unwilling, they forced themselves to read it to the end; one said pompously that this year's list was quite fair; one said that his dream on New Year's Eve had come true; and another one said that he hadn't been satisfied with his essay.

Later, someone who had made a clean copy of the first-place essay sat in the balcony of a wine shop reading it, his head swaying back and forth. A young man beside him asked, "Why is it so short?"

The one who was reading said, "The essay is long—I chose only his best phrases to copy. Come here and we'll read it together. You can learn some of his methods and pass next year." The two of them began to read in a clear voice:

The revitalized lost vocation, reestablished human relations, the true vista in learning, the perfect spirit in government—what are these? This sphere is, like Hun-tun,[5] irretrievable. This principle is, like breathing, indispensable. Therefore, the sperm of original nature has never issued forth; even the ashes of written books maintain spirituality. In a word, the primal act of creation should not be seen as below the mean, and the secret motivations of the spirits can easily be pinched between two fingers.

Monkey burst out laughing and said, "Five hundred years ago when I was in the Eight Trigrams Cauldron,[6] I overheard Lao-tzu talking with the Jade-history Immortal about the destiny of literature. He said, 'From the time of Yao and Shun to Confucius[7] was the Cycle of Pure Heaven. That may be called great abundance. From Mencius to Li Ssu[8] was the Pure Earth Cycle and can be called middle abundance. The five hundred years since has been the Water and Thunder Cycle. The body of literature has been vast but its vitality has fallen short. This may be called the small decline. Eight hundred years hence it will turn to the Mountain-water Cycle. Things will be rotten! Rotten!'

"The Jade-history Immortal asked why it would be so bad. Lao-tzu replied, 'Alas, a bunch of earless, eyeless, tongueless, noseless, handless, legless, heartless, lungless, boneless, muscleless, bloodless, and spiritless people will be called "outstanding scholars." In the hundred years of their lives, they will only use up one sheet of paper, and after their coffin lids are nailed shut, no two lines they wrote will be remembered. Their writings will be far from the truth. Though Hun-tun will have been dead for several myriad years, they won't let him lie. Rather than letting Yao and Shun sit in their Yellow Palace in peace, they'll insist on dragging them in. Breathing is a pure and empty thing, but instead of nourishing the breath they'll hinder it. The spirit is the treasure of the body, but instead of calming it they'll stir it up. What do you think this kind of literature is called? It's called "gauze-hat[9] writing." If they happen to write a few sentences, it will be their good fortune, because then others will support them, flatter them, and fear them.'

---

[5] Hun-tun is the primal undifferentiated state before the phenomenal universe came into being, often personified, as in Lao-tzu's speech below.

[6] In chapter 7 of *Journey to the West* Lao-tzu attempted to melt Monkey in his alchemical Eight Trigrams Cauldron after other efforts to dispose of Monkey had failed.

[7] I.e., from the time of the sage-emperors, traditionally placed in approximately the twenty-third century B.C., to Confucius (551–479 B.C.).

[8] Mencius (385?–289? B.C.) and Li Ssu (280–208 B.C.).

[9] The gauze-hat is the silk hat worn as insignia of official or noble status.

"By the time Lao-tzu had finished speaking, the Jade-history Immortal was in tears and left. When I remember this exchange, it's clear that the number one essay belongs to the Mountain-water Cycle.

"But what do I care, anyway?' Let me take a look at the second mirror under 'Heaven.'"

CHAPTER FIVE

Through the Cast Bronze Mirror the Mind-Monkey Enters the Past;
In Green Pearl's Tower the Wayward Disciple Knits His Brows.

Monkey turned to gaze into the second mirror under the character "Heaven," an antique cast bronze mirror. There under a great cypress tree stood a stone tablet on which twelve characters were carved in seal script saying: "The World of the Ancients was originally neighbor to the Headache World."

Monkey said, "Since it's the World of the Ancients, the First Emperor of Ch'in must be in there. The other day that concubine sweeping in the New T'ang palace said he possessed a Mountain-removing Bell. I'll grab him and take his bell, then I'll sweep away the thousand mountains and ten thousand gorges from the road to the Western Paradise. The monsters and robbers will have no place to hide."

He thereupon changed himself into a bronze-drilling insect, climbed onto the face of the mirror, and got ready. He bit out one mouthful, then bored through the mirror.

All at once he fell into a high pavilion. Hearing several people below, he didn't dare show his real self, but remained in the form of a drilling insect and hid in the crack of a window covered in green flowers.

It so happened that in the World of the Ancients there was a beautiful lady called Green Pearl.[1] Day in and day out she treated her guests to banquets with drinking games and the chanting of poems. After planning for a long while she had a hundred-foot-tall pavilion built and called it the Fragrance-gripping Pavilion. Just that day Lady Hsi-shih[2] and

---

[1] Green Pearl was the beautiful concubine of the rich and extravagant Shih Ch'ung of the Chin dynasty (264–419) who purchased her for fifteen pecks of pearls.

[2] Hsi-shih was a famous beauty who lived in the state of Yüeh during the Spring and Autumn Period (722–481 B.C.). She was sent by King Kou-chien of Yüeh to King Fu-ch'ai of Wu and later caused the collapse of the state of Wu. According to one legend, on

Miss Silk[3] had come together to congratulate Green Pearl on the new pavilion.

Green Pearl was delighted. She immediately had a banquet spread in the pavilion for them to join her in sisterly affection. Miss Silk sat in the middle; Green Pearl sat to her right and Lady Hsi-shih to her left. A number of maid servants attended the ladies: some served wine, some picked flowers, and some held the dice bowls.

Monkey, still in the window, decided to play a prank. He changed into a maid-servant and sneaked inconspicuously into their midst. How did he look?

Top-knot like the Goddess of the River Lo,[4]
Eyebrows of Chu Hsiao-chi.
The king of Ch'u[5] *loved a waist like that,*
The emperor of Han, a robe.
Above, autumn-wind earrings,
Below, lotus-flower cups.[6]

Then the maids-in-waiting began to giggle and said, "Our Fragrance-gripping Pavilion truly snatches up fragrance. Even though this beautiful girl doesn't live here, she came right in."

Another maid said to Monkey, "Have you seen Lady Green Pearl, sister?"

Monkey said, "Elder sister, I'm new here. Could you take me to meet her?"

The maid giggled and led Monkey to meet Lady Green Pearl. Green Pearl looked shocked. With tears in her eyes she said to Monkey, "Beautiful Lady Yü,[7] I haven't seen you for so long! But why is your fair face so sad?"

---

the way from Yüeh to Wu, Hsi-shih became romantically involved with the diplomat Fan Li who presented her to the King of Wu.

[3] We are not able to identify Miss Silk.

[4] The daughter of the ancient mythical emperor Fu-hsi drowned herself in the River Lo and became its goddess.

[5] King Ling of Ch'u loved girls with slim waists.

[6] I.e., the shoes worn on a lady's delicate bound feet.

[7] Beautiful Lady Yü was the favorite concubine of Hsiang Yü, Hegemon of Ch'u, a leader of the rebellion that ended the Ch'in dynasty in 207 B.C. After wiping out the last Ch'in emperor's family and setting fire to the capital of Hsien-yang, he parceled the empire into separate states over which he exercised hegemony from the state of Ch'u. Shortly

Monkey was surprised to hear this and thought, "Since I was born from a stone egg, I've never been reincarnated by way of any parents, and I've never chased the mists and flowers. When did I know this Lady Green Pearl? Since when am I Beautiful Lady Mud, Beautiful Lady Copper, Beautiful Lady Iron, or Beautiful Lady Grass? But that's what she calls me. Well, what do I care if I'm Beautiful Lady Yü or not? I'll play the role for a little while—it should be amusing. This is called meeting one error with another.

"Just one thing—since I've become Beautiful Lady Yü, I must have a husband somewhere. If she asks about him and my answer turns out to be a case of 'a horse's jaw not matching an ass's head,' it'll show my true colors. I'll sound her out a bit and find out about my 'husband,' then I can join in the banquet."

Green Pearl called again, "Beautiful Lady! Quick, have a seat! Although what's in the cup is weak, it will chase away your gloom."

Monkey put on a long face and said to Green Pearl, "Sister, people say wine cheers the joyful heart, but my husband and I can't see each other. The silken strands of rain and gusts of wind have long pierced and broken my heart. How can I swallow wine?"

Green Pearl started and said, "But my dear lady, what are you saying? Your husband is Hsiang Yü, Hegemon of Ch'u. You live together—why can't you see each other?"

Catching the five words "Hsiang Yü, Hegemon of Ch'u," Monkey answered off the top of his head, "Sister, you don't know that the Hegemon of Ch'u of today is not the same man as before. There is a concubine named Sorrow of Ch'u who uses her many charms to entice my husband and separate the two of us.

"Once we were walking in the moonlight and, when I didn't look at the water weeds in the pond, she purposely leaned on the railing as if lost in thought. My husband said, 'The way she gazes is so lovely.'

"Another time we were looking at flowers and I didn't call for wine. She went to her room and got a pot with a cracked ice design containing Purple Flower Jade Dew wine. She offered it and said, 'Long life to my gracious lord,' and just as she left, she winked at him seductively. My husband saw her off with a twinkle in his eye. I have nothing but love for him—my only wish is that we could always be a pair of mandarin ducks. When I saw those two putting me on a closet shelf, how could I be anything but sad and resentful?

---

thereafter, he was destroyed by his vassal, King of Han (Liu Pang), who went on to found the Han dynasty (206 B.C.–A.D. 220).

"Then my husband complained that I didn't pay any attention to him and, what's more, that Sorrow of Ch'u had been trying hard to please. He took his sword and scabbard from under the bed, and slung them across his back. He didn't even call for any of his men but just left looking straight ahead. I don't know where he went. That was twenty days ago—more than half a month and not a word from him." And Monkey began to wail.

When Green Pearl saw this, her tears soaked half her silken sleeve. Hsi-shih and Miss Silk sighed together. Even the maids carrying the wine pots felt tears fill their throats and sympathetic pains in their hearts. It's a fact that a sad person shouldn't talk to other sad people—if they do, they only become sadder.

The four of them sat down and Hsi-shih said, "Our Beautiful Lady isn't happy tonight and we three should try to cheer her up. We mustn't add to her sadness." So saying, she produced six dice and held them in her hands. She called out, "Sisters of this banquet, hear my command! If the first throw doesn't show a one, each of us will chant a line of old-style verse. If the second throw doesn't throw a two, we must all confess our sexual fancies. If the third throw doesn't show a three, I will punish myself with one big cup, then pass it to one of you."

Hsi-shih looked up and threw the dice and shouted, "There's no one on the first throw!"

Green Pearl trilled a line of poetry in a sweet voice: "When my husband doesn't come, the cold night is long."

Miss Silk laughed in great admiration and said, "The double-meaning in this line is magnificent." She also chanted a line: "The Jade Lady's earrings dangle in the autumn wind."

Monkey thought, "Now it's my turn. I can remember several lines of other kinds of writing, but thinking of poetry makes my head ache. What's more, I don't know if Beautiful Lady Yü knows poetry or not. If she doesn't, I'll be all right; if she does, I'll give myself away."

Green Pearl said, "A line, please, Beautiful Lady." Monkey answered evasively, "I can't write poetry."

Hsi-shih laughed and said, "*The Selected Poems of the Beautiful Lady* has circulated throughout the Central Plain. Even tiny children know that Beautiful Lady Yü is talented in composing *tz'u*- and *fu*-style poetry. And here today you're acting coy!"

Monkey had no choice but to raise his face and seek inspiration. He was lost in thought a long while, then asked the group, "Is it all right if I don't use a line from an ancient poet?"

Green Pearl said, "You'll have to ask our leader."

Monkey asked Hsi-shih and she said, "What difference does it make? Once you compose a line, it'll be the same as one from the ancients!"

Everyone inclined her ear to listen and Monkey chanted a line: "I regret my heart follows clouds and rain in flight."

Green Pearl asked Miss Silk, "What do you think of the Beautiful Lady's line?"

Miss Silk replied, "Who would dare say the Beautiful Lady's poetry is not good? Only this line somehow smacks of monkishness."

Hsi-shih laughed and said, "The Beautiful Lady was once a nun for half a month."

Monkey said, "Oh, don't tease. Would you please pass the dice bowl on?"

Hsi-shih quickly handed the dice bowl to Green Pearl, who lifted her hand and tossed the dice. She shouted, "The second throw doesn't show a two!"

Hsi-shih said, "It's easy for you to confess but hard for me."

Green Pearl asked, "But sister, what's so hard for you to confess?"

Hsi-shih exclaimed, "Hmph! You're trying to embarrass me! You must know I've had two husbands!"

Green Pearl persisted, "Even though we have different names we're all your flesh and blood. What harm is there in it? I've got an idea—why don't you give us a line about King Wu and then one about young Fan?"

Hsi-shih heard this and straightaway confessed:

Young Fan: Green years on Willow Stream.
King Wu: Rosy cheeks in a jade palace.
Young Fan: Vowed to the sun on K'un-lun Mountains.
King Wu: Slept the night beneath a wu-t'ung tree.
Young Fan: Lamented the moon on Five Lakes.
King Wu: Grieved day-long once drunk.

After hearing this, Green Pearl tipped her cup and made her own confession:

I have a peck of pearls;
Ten-thousand piculs of tears.
Tonight in Fragrance-gripping Pavilion;
Another year in Snow-spread Hall.

Green Pearl sighed with each word. Hsi-shih said in a loud voice, "Penalty! I wanted you to tell about delights, but instead you tell about sorrows!"

Green Pearl admitted her guilt and accepted a wine penalty. Meanwhile Miss Silk tried to get Monkey to go next, while Monkey deferred to her. They bandied back and forth, but neither would confess. Finally Green Pearl said, "I've got another idea. Sister Silk, you say one line, and then you say one, Beautiful Lady."

Hsi-shih said, "That can't be done. Hegemon Ch'u has a valiant and heroic air. Young Shen is fair of face, gentle and warm. How could they be put together?"

Miss Silk laughed and said, "It's all right. She is she and I am I. Let me confess first." And she said, "Weep for the moon in South Tower."

Without thinking, Monkey said, "Worship Buddha in the Western Paradise."

Green Pearl pointed at Monkey and said, "I think you must be confused, Beautiful Lady. Why do you bring up worshipping Buddha in the Western Paradise?"

Monkey said, "My words are profound and want explication. 'Paradise' means 'husband'; 'Western' stands for 'Western Ch'u'; 'worship' means 'return' and 'Buddha' means 'heart.' So what it means is, 'My heart returns to my husband in Western Ch'u.' Although he dislikes me, I think only of him."

Green Pearl breathed a long sigh of admiration.

Monkey feared that if he stayed too long at the banquet it would delay his journey, so he pretended he was drunk and about to throw up.

Hsi-shih said, "Let's not have a third throw. Let's go look at the moon."

The four of them left the banquet and walked downstairs. They stepped aimlessly over some wild flowers and disported themselves with some water weeds. Monkey, wanting only to find the First Emperor of Ch'in, thought up a plan to get away. "I have a pain in my heart. I can't bear it ... can't bear it—please let me go home," he moaned.

Green Pearl said, "Heart pains are ordinary things for us. Don't you worry, I'll have someone ask Dr. Ch'i Po to come and take your pulse."

Monkey said, "No, that won't do. These days doctors are the last people I want around. All they can do is make a live man dead and small ills big. When it comes to healing, they only want quick results—they don't care about your body. And if your humors are unbalanced, they make you take ginseng, and then you suffer for it the rest of your life. I still want to go home."

Green Pearl said, "If you go home and don't see Hegemon Ch'u, you'll get depressed again, and if you see Sorrow of Ch'u, your hatred will start all over again. People with heart pain should avoid depression and hatred."

The "sisters" all tried to persuade Monkey to stay, but Monkey insisted that he wouldn't. Seeing that the illness was serious and that she couldn't make her stay, Green Pearl could only ask four of her personal maids to escort Beautiful Lady Yü home.

Monkey put on a sleepy face, clasped his hands over his breast, and took leave of the "sisters." Supported by the four maids, he descended the hundred-foot Fragrance-gripping Pavilion. As they walked toward the main road, Monkey said, "You four go on back. Be sure to say thanks for me, and tell your mistress and my 'little sister' we'll get together again tomorrow."

The maids said, "Just a moment ago when we left, Lady Green Pearl instructed us to accompany you all the way to Hegemon Ch'u's estate."

Monkey said, "So you don't want to return, eh? See my cudgel!"

No sooner had he spoken than the cudgel was in his hand. With one full-power sweep, the four maids were beaten to red powder.

Monkey returned to his real form. He raised his head to look around and found himself directly in front of Nü-kua's[8] gate. He was pleased and said, "Heaven was chopped open by Little Moon King's sky-gougers, and yesterday they put the blame on me. Although Lao-tzu is obnoxious and the Jade Emperor stupid, I made a mistake, too. I shouldn't have done something five hundred years ago to start tongues wagging. Still, I'm not going to surrender myself now.

"I've heard that Nü-kua has had long experience in patching heaven. I'll ask her to fix it for me today and then go crying up to the Palace of Magic Mists and wash myself clean. This is really a great opportunity."

He walked up to the gate for a better look, but all he saw were two black doors shut tight. The doors were sealed with a piece of paper that said: "Went to the Yellow Emperor's for a chat on the twentieth. Back in ten days. Sorry, honorable visitor. I extend my apologies here in advance."

---

[8] Nü-kua was a younger sister of the sage-emperor Fu-hsi, mythical author of the *I Ching* (*Book of Changes*). She was supposed to have had the head of a woman and a serpent's body and to have repaired heaven after it was knocked from its supporting pillars during a war.

Monkey read this and turned to go. He heard the cock crow three times. It was nearly dawn. He had traveled several million miles and still hadn't seen the First Emperor of Ch'in.

CHAPTER SIX

For a Face Half Covered with Tears, the True Beauty Dies;
At the Mention of P'ing-hsiang, the General of Ch'u Is Grieved.

All of a sudden Monkey noticed a dark man sitting in a high pavilion. Monkey laughed and said, "So there are rebels in the World of the Ancients, too! His whole face has been blackened with coal and he's on public exhibit here."

He advanced a few steps, then said, "No, he's no rebel; it's a temple for Chang Fei."[1] But after thinking it over he said, "If it were Chang Fei's temple, he'd wear a turban. Even if there's a new style, at most he'd be wearing a general's helmet—an emperor's crown can't be worn by just anyone. Since he's wearing a crown and his face is dark, this must be Great Yü,[2] the Dark Emperor. I'll go see him and ask his secret method for controlling monsters and killing demons. Then I won't have to bother looking for the First Emperor of Ch'in."

As he neared the front of the pavilion, he saw that below the platform stood a stone column, from the top of which flew a white banner. The banner had seven words written in purple saying, "The Famous Pre-Han Knight, Hsiang Yü."

When Monkey read this he laughed aloud and said, "That just goes to show you shouldn't think about things that haven't happened—when you think about them, they won't turn out the way you expect. Here I speculated this way and that, saying he was Great Yü, the Dark Emperor, or Chang Fei, or a rebel—who'd have thought he'd be none other than my 'husband' from Green Pearl's tower."

He thought a bit more and said, "Wait a minute—I drilled into this World of the Ancients to find the First Emperor of Ch'in and borrow his

---

[1] Chang Fei was a general of the Kingdom of Shu during the Three Kingdoms period (A.D. 220–280). He is usually depicted with a black face.

[2] Great Yü was the legendary sage-emperor who quelled the Great Flood.

51

Mountain-removing Bell. The Hegemon of Ch'u, whom I just saw, lived after him. Why haven't I seen the First Emperor? I've got an idea— I'll climb the pavilion to see Hsiang Yü and ask him for information about the First Emperor. Then I can figure out where he is."

Monkey jumped up for a closer look. He saw that below the pavilion there was an area with green grass, red railings, flowers here and there, and bird song everywhere. There sat a beautiful lady. Monkey heard someone call, "Beautiful Lady Yü! Beautiful Lady Yü!"

Monkey laughed and said, "Well, well. Old Monkey from Green Pearl's tower is here now. What's it to me if this Lady Yü is dead or alive?"

Monkey gave his body a shake and, as before, changed himself into a likeness of the beautiful lady. He climbed the pavilion, took out a long white handkerchief, and began to daub at tears. With only half his face showing, he looked at Hsiang Yü as if resentful and angry.

Hsiang Yü was startled and fell to his knees. Monkey turned his back. Hsiang Yü flew over to kneel in front of Monkey and said, "Beautiful Lady, have pity on your bedfellow! Please, a little smile!"

When Monkey didn't respond, Hsiang Yü could do nothing but tear up in sympathy. Then Monkey's face became red as a peach blossom. He pointed at Hsiang Yü and said, "Stupid thief! A feared general like you can't even protect a girl! How can you have the face to sit on this high platform?"

Hsiang Yü only blubbered and didn't dare reply. Monkey put on a look of pity. He helped him up and said, "It's often said there's yellow gold on a man's knees. After this you really mustn't kneel without call."

Hsiang Yü said, "What are you saying, Beautiful Lady? When I saw you knit your sorrowful brows, my heart and lungs were crushed. What do I care about my body? What did you mean by what you said?"

Monkey said, "I can't keep it from you, Your Majesty. I was feeling a bit ill, and slept on the rattan couch for half an hour. But then I saw a monkey spirit jump out of the magnolia tree outside the window. He claimed to be the Great Sage Equal to Heaven and the Bodhisattva Sun Wu-k'ung, the one who caused a ruckus in the Heavenly Palace five hundred years ago."

When Hsiang Yü heard this he leapt to his feet and shouted "Get my sword from the headboard of the jade bed! Get my sword! If you can't find the sword bring the tiger-head spear."

Then he scratched his head, stamped his feet, and bellowed, "Where is he now?"

Monkey leaned over and said, "You needn't get so excited, Your Majesty. Don't get so angry that you hurt yourself. Let me tell you slowly. That ape was disgusting. He came up beside the couch and flirted lewdly with me. Though I'm not bright, how could I be so stupid as to mistake adultery for chastity?

"I shouted for the maids but didn't know the ape had said a charm to freeze them in their tracks. I knew something was wrong when I couldn't get a single maid to come. I flung down my round fan and straightened my gown. The ape glared at me. Then he grabbed me and threw me into the Blossom Rain Tower, then turned and jumped away.

"I was terrified in the Blossom Rain Tower, but I stole a glance to see where he'd gone. What do you think he did, Your Majesty? He went and sat on my flower-shaded rattan couch, changed into my likeness, and called for the maids. I'm afraid that in a little while he'll try to delude Your Majesty.

"I'm not worth troubling over—I'm just afraid that Your Majesty won't be able to tell the true from the false and will fall into poisonous hands. My crying was only for you, Your Majesty."

When Hsiang Yü heard this, he took the sword in his right hand and the spear in his left and screamed "Kill him!" He leapt from the pavilion and charged to the flower-shaded couch. There he cut off Beautiful Lady Yü's head and threw it, dripping with blood, into the lotus pond.

He told all the maids, "Don't cry. This was a false lady, so I killed her. The real lady is in my pavilion."

Holding back their tears, the maids quickly followed King Hsiang to the pavilion. When they saw Monkey they changed from sad to happy and said, "Our true lady is indeed here. It nearly scared us maids to death."

King Hsiang was very happy. To the maids he said, "Sweep the Blossom Rain Tower. And carefully prepare some wine: first to calm the lady's nerves and second to celebrate my joy over killing the monster and dispelling doubt." The maids below the pavilion answered, "Yes, Your Majesty," in one voice. Meanwhile the maids in the pavilion came to soothe Monkey's breast and stroke his back. They offered tea and water, and some asked, "Were you afraid, Madam? Is your heart still thumping?"

Monkey said, "A little."

One asked, "You didn't fall and hurt your lower body, did you?"

Monkey said, "No, I didn't. It's just that this gasping for breath is hard to bear."

King Hsiang said, "Gasping for breath isn't serious. Just calm down and sit for a while—you'll be all right."

Suddenly a couple of maids knelt before the king and the lady and said, "Your Majesty, My Lady, please come to the feast."

Monkey said to himself, "I shouldn't do everything he says yet." He pretended to be seized by an evil spirit, and with his two eyes staring blankly at the king he said, "Give me back my head!"

King Hsiang was alarmed and said again and again, "Beautiful Lady! Beautiful Lady!"

Monkey didn't respond, but rolled his eyes back till only the whites showed. King Hsiang said, "This has got to be Sun Wu-k'ung's ghost—it hasn't dispersed yet and has taken possession of Beautiful Lady's body. Quick! Get the yellow-robed Taoist priest to exorcise the spirit. Then she'll be all right."

A little while later two maids and the Taoist priest mounted the pavilion. The Taoist carried a bell and spat magic water from his mouth. He chanted a spell:

In the time of the Three Emperors, there were the Yellow Emperor, Hsüan Yüan, and the Divine Lord, Great Shun. Great Shun's name was Yü. Hsüan-yüan's family name was Kung-sun. Sun Yü and Yü Sun were originally related through marriage, but today there's been a feud—when will it be settled? I kowtow to your valiant spirit, Honorable Monk and Great Sage, Mr. Sun. Fly quickly to the upper regions and start another row in the Heavenly Palace. Release Beautiful Lady Yü and seek the T'ang Priest. Quick! Quick! Follow my orders. Otherwise this Taoist priest will gain no merit and a Buddhist monk will have to come.

Monkey called out, "Taoist Priest! Do you know who I am?"

The priest knelt and said, "A thousand years to you, My Lady."

Monkey scolded, "Taoist Priest! Really! You can't get rid of me! I'm the Great Sage Equal of Heaven! I have a score to settle and I possessed her body to do it. Today is an auspicious day. I'm determined to marry Beautiful Lady Yü. Why don't you act as go-between? It'll be worth your while—you'll get the go-between's fee." After that he yelled some more gibberish.

The Taoist priest's limbs went numb. He could only hold his sword before him and wave it feebly back and forth. He meekly spat half a mouthful of magic water and chanted in a low voice, "Make haste to follow the order of the Supreme Lord Lao-tzu." But there was no response.

Monkey was secretly sorry for the priest, so after a while he made his eyes look alive again. He called out, "Your Majesty ... dear Husband ... Where are you?"

King Hsiang was greatly pleased. He immediately gave the priest a hundred taels of white gold and sent him back to the temple. Then he hurried over to help Monkey to his feet and said, "Beautiful Lady, why did you frighten me so?"

Monkey said, "I don't know. I only saw that Monkey coming near my couch again, and then I felt dizzy. When he took that mouthful of magic water from the Taoist priest, he couldn't stand steady, then he ran off in the direction of the southwest. But now my head is very clear—let's go and drink some wine."

King Hsiang took Monkey's hand. They walked down from the pavilion and went to sit in the Blossom Rain Tower. There phoenix-lamps cast their brilliance, cinnamon candles flickered, and the maids all stood in rows.

After several rounds of wine, Monkey suddenly stood up and said to Hsiang Yü, "Your Majesty, I want to sleep."

Hsiang Yü quickly called, "Maid P'ing-hsiang! Light the candles." The two of them went into the bedroom holding hands. They had a cup of tea from Mount Chieh and sat side-by-side on the couch. Monkey thought, "If I leave now, I won't get any information about the First August Emperor of Ch'in. But what if I go inside the bed curtains with him and he makes some move? Should I let him or not? I'd be better off finding a way to escape." And he said to Hsiang Yü, "Your Majesty, there's something I've been meaning to say to you, but there's been so much going on that every time I see you I forget. Ever since I've been with you, I've hoped to have children to carry on after us forever. Who would have thought that these several years there'd be no results? And also, Your Majesty, you love only me and haven't had to look around for concubines. Now the snow drifts in your locks and your body's grown plump. Although I'm not clever I secretly fear you'll become a lonely man, and that when you die you'll be a ghost without an heir. The maid P'ing-hsiang has natural beauty and supple grace; her eyes embrace a man like mist. I've sounded out her literary taste several times and find her quite sensitive. Why doesn't Your Majesty call her to serve you tonight?"

The color drained from King Hsiang's face and he said, "Beautiful Lady, I think today's shock must have tipped your heart. Why should such a jealous person as you say such an unjealous thing?"

Monkey smiled and said, "Your Majesty, it's only for your own good that I'm not usually so tolerant. Now I give you my leave for the sake of your sons and grandsons. My heart isn't tipped. I only hope that in the future your heart won't become slanted."

King Hsiang said, "Beautiful Lady, even if you asked me ten thousand times, I wouldn't dare to take P'ing-hsiang. Have you forgotten so soon that five years ago on the fifteenth of the first month, the time of the Lantern Festival, we vowed to share life and death together? Now you're teasing me."

Monkey saw that it wouldn't work. He smiled again and said, "Your Majesty, I only fear you might forsake me. How could I ever forsake you? But now there's something else that might upset you."

CHAPTER SEVEN

Four Drumbeats Between Ch'in and Ch'u;
Beautiful Ladies, True and False, Appear in the Same Mirror.

Hsiang Yü asked Beautiful Lady Yü, "What is it?"

Monkey said, "The shock I had from that ape today upset my heart and blood. Perhaps Your Majesty would enter the silk curtain of mutual happiness first? I'll stay here on the couch and rest a while. I'd also like to have some green tea and wait 'til the depression in my heart eases. Then I'll come to bed."

Hsiang Yü embraced Monkey and said, "How could I leave you and go to sleep alone? If you don't go to bed till the first watch, I'll stay up till the first watch. If you don't go to bed all night, I'll stay up all night.

"Beautiful Lady," he continued, "I've had too many cups of wine tonight. My insides are knotted in a World of Grief. Let me tell you some stories to keep you company and calm myself too."

Monkey giggled and said, "I hope Your Majesty will control your temper and talk slowly."

King Hsiang assumed an air of forbearance and impassioned indignation to deliver his story, grasping his scabbard with one hand and placing his left foot forward. He began: "Beautiful Lady, Beautiful Lady, my life is complete! This Hsiang Yü is a true man. Until I was twenty I hadn't studied calligraphy or swordsmanship. When I saw how stupid the Ch'in Emperor was, I led eight thousand men and took along the seventy-two year old Fan Tseng[1] with the one intention of replacing the Ch'in Emperor. At that time there was a Taoist in a feathered robe who knew the workings of the cosmos. Several times I sent men to see him, and each time he said Ch'in's mandate had not run out.

"Beautiful Lady, do you think Ch'in's mandate had really expired or not? Later my power waxed strong and my ambition was fierce. Even

---

[1] Fan Tseng was an old and wise strategist who helped Hsiang Yü establish hegemony.

good old Heaven was no longer in control. Ch'in shouldn't have ended, but it did; Ch'u shouldn't have risen, but it did.

"One morning I hung up Sung I's[2] head, reeking of blood. The courage of all the generals took flight and they stood with their tongues hanging and knees shaking. Those days it was great fun being Hsiang Yü.

"When Chang Han[3] came to do battle, I went out to meet him. The strength of the Ch'in army was still great then. A general rode in front of my horse and I shouted at him, 'What's your name?' When he saw my dark face and heard my rumbling voice, he fell from his silver dappled horse with a thud. I spared that one.

"Then came another general. On his fluttering red banner was clearly written, 'Great Ch'in General Huang Chang.' I thought, 'If Ch'in has come to this, it's no longer great,' and let out a laugh, 'Ha! Ha! Ha!' on the battlefield. I wouldn't have guessed that the sight of my laughing face would crush his bones to powder. His spear hung limp and half his body sagged; frantic, he waved a signal banner and beat a green metal gong. Then I saw a general in gold armor rushing away toward his own camp.

"By then I was on the edge of the Ch'in encampment. I lost my temper and taunted Chang Han: 'Little Ch'in general, you don't dare stick your own head out! Instead you send out these three- or four-inch high babies carrying wooden sticks to offer themselves to my sword.'

"Then the blade of my precious sword said to me, 'I don't want to drink the blood of those little lackeys—I want Chang Han's blood!' I heeded the words of my precious sword and let Huang Chang go.

"Beautiful Lady, what kind of man do you think Chang Han was? It was already sunset and that lackey Chang Han was leading ten thousand crack troops. He didn't open his mouth, didn't say a word. He picked up a jade-handled mountain-cleaving axe and swung it at my head. My whole body was aflame and my precious blade began to hum. One of my aides, Kao San-ch'u, seemed to me a man of ambitious mettle. He said, 'Chang Han must not be killed. He should be made to surrender. I need a cook in my camp—give the job to Chang Han.'

"I listened to Kao San-ch'u's suggestion and lightly swung the tip of my sword, killed the dappled dragon-horse he rode, and sent him away with Kao. Was Chang Han ever scared!"

---

[2] Sung I was one of the generals who led the rebellion against the Ch'in. He was killed by Hsiang Yü.

[3] Chang Han was a great general of Ch'in whose defeat by Hsiang Yü signaled the collapse of the dynasty.

Monkey said in a low voice, "Have some tea, Your Majesty, then you can slowly tell me more."

No sooner had Hsiang Yü stopped speaking than they heard a "thump ... thump ... " sound from the guard tower. It was the second watch. Hsiang Yü said, "Beautiful Lady, don't you want to sleep?"

Monkey said, "My heart is still depressed."

Hsiang Yü said, "Since you won't sleep, I'll go on with the story. Next morning at daybreak I was still snoring 'zza-zza' in my tiger-head tent when I heard a million men shouting from the south, 'Ten thousand years! Ten thousand years!' From the north a million shouted 'Ten thousand years! Ten thousand years!' From the west a million shouted, 'Ten thousand years!' and from the east another million shouted, 'Ten thousand years!' I rolled over in bed and asked the orderly, 'I suppose that's the Emperor of Ch'in, who's led his soldiers out to fight me? Since he's also an emperor I'll put on a new suit of armor today.'

"Beautiful Lady, what do you think the orderly said? He knelt beside my tent and said with a stutter, 'Y-Your M-M-Majesty is mistaken; are you still using the word "Ch'in" today? The lords from the eight directions stand before Your Majesty's jade tent and shout "Ten thousand years!"'

"Hearing him say this I quickly combed my hair and put on my helmet, washed my feet and put on my shoes, but I didn't bother to put on new armor. I gave orders at once calling all the lords under Heaven to come through the gate and hear me speak. My order was given at 9:00 a.m. Twelve o'clock passed. One o'clock passed. But the lords outside the gate had not yet come in. I began to have doubts. I told the orderly to go out and ask the lords, 'Since you want to see me, come in on the double! Do you expect me to come out and see you?'

"I was going to say something more when the gates of the camp were suddenly thrown wide open. I saw all the world's kings and lords all shortened by one half! I was shocked and the color left my face. I thought to myself, 'Why do these heroes have only half a body each?' When I looked closely, I saw they were using their knees as feet and crawling step-by-step up the stairs. Before my tent and to the right, several people wearing crowns and pearled robes knelt face down, and to the left knelt still others.

"I was just about to reproach them and say, 'Why did it take you so long to come in after I called?' when my aides reported, 'Your Majesty, when all the lords now at the foot of the steps received Your Majesty's orders, they assembled for a conference in front of your tent. They didn't dare walk through the gate standing up. They didn't dare merely salute with folded hands, nor did they dare appear disorderly. They discussed it among themselves, then fell prostrate on the ground and didn't move. They talked it over—they were sad and anxious, worried and depressed, frantic and bewildered. Finally 'they decided on a "knee-walking method"; only then did they dare come to meet you.'

"When I heard this I had a bit of compassion and called out, 'You lords of all the earth, raise up your heads!' Who do you think dared to move his head or legs? I only heard a rumbling from the ground. It wasn't the sound of a bell or drum or gold-ringed reed whistle. When I listened carefully, it turned out that the lords were still saying, 'Ten thousand years!' They continued to kowtow and did not dare lift their heads. Thinking back on it, that was a great year for Hsiang Yü."

Monkey made a sound like a flower falling on an empty stairway and said, "Your Majesty, you must be exhausted, have a little green bean broth. Wait a bit and then go on with the story." Just as Hsiang Yü stopped speaking, the drum in the guard tower was sounded three times. Monkey said, "It's the third watch."

Hsiang Yü said, "Beautiful Lady, your heart-sickness hasn't yet passed. Allow me to continue the story.

"After this, the Lord of P'ei[4] was disrespectful and put me off a bit, but I ignored him and entered the Land-within-the-Passes. I saw a man ten miles off, conspicuous in a crown studded with pearls and jade, like the sun, moon, and stars. He wore an elegant robe with mountains, dragons and water weeds embroidered upon it and rode a rich chariot painted green and blue and carved with phoenixes among coiled dragons. His retinue of officials carrying silver and gold seals and draped in yellow robes with purple sashes numbered several thousand. They marched in a serpentine column that stretched into the far distance. When they saw me through the pines, the man in front quickly removed his sun-moon-star jade and pearl crown and put on a commoner's hempen cap. He took off his mountain-dragon-water weed embroidered robe and put on a somber green and white robe. He got down from the green and blue dragon and phoenix chariot and clasped his hands behind his back. The officials carrying silver and gold seals and wearing yellow robes and purple sashes all changed into grass sandals and wooden belts and painted their faces red. They fell to their knees and prostrated themselves on the ground, wishing they could go several thousand or ten thousand feet into the ground.

---

[4] I.e., Liu Pang, founder of the Han dynasty.

"When they were thus properly dressed, I galloped up to them on my dark dappled horse. On all sides I heard 'Ten thousand years to our Lord! Ten thousand years to our Lord!' I glanced out of the corner of my eyes and the leader again said, 'Ten thousand years to our Lord—I am King Tzu-ying of Ch'in[5] and am come to surrender to you.'

"In those days I was quick-tempered and my arm was swift. One swipe of my sword—'whoosh!'—made them all, king and official, young and old, headless ghosts. Those were good times.

"I shouted, 'Ghost of the First Emperor of Ch'in, you should have expected this day!'"

As it happened that Monkey's mind was intent on seeking the First Emperor of Ch'in, he pretended to collapse when Hsiang Yü came out with the name and said, "Your Majesty, don't say any more. I want to sleep."

When Hsiang Yü heard Beautiful Lady Yü say she wished to sleep, what could he do but agree? He forthwith shut his mouth. They heard the guard tower drum beat "thump . . . thump . . . thump . . . thump . . . thump"—in the fifth watch. Monkey said, "Your Majesty, the last part of the story was really long. We missed the drum for the fourth watch."

Monkey laid down on the couch, and Hsiang Yü, too, laid down and shared the pillow. Monkey said to Hsiang Yü, "I can't sleep, Your Majesty."

Hsiang Yü said, "Since Beautiful Lady can't sleep, I'll tell more of the story."

Monkey said, "It's all right for you to tell stories, but this time don't say such shameless words."

Hsiang Yü said, "What do you mean, 'shameless words'?"

Monkey said, "There's no shame in talking about others, but talking about oneself is shameless. Let me ask you, where is the First Emperor of Ch'in now?"

Hsiang Yü said, "Ah, the First Emperor was also quite a man. Except for one thing—where other men were complacent, he was foolish."

Monkey said, "He conquered six states and built the Great Wall. He must have been an intelligent man."

Hsiang Yü said, "Beautiful Lady, one must distinguish intelligent foolishness from foolish intelligence. The First Emperor's intelligence is foolish intelligence. His Primal Celestial Excellency saw that the Emperor

---

[5] King Tzu-ying was the second and last successor of the First Emperor of Ch'in. He abandoned the imperial title and reverted to the title of king.

was intensely oblivious and didn't belong in the World of the Ancients, so he sent him to the World of Oblivion."

Monkey caught the words "World of Oblivion" but they didn't mean anything to him. He quickly asked, "How far is the World of Oblivion from here?"

Hsiang Yü said, "The World of the Future lies in between."

Monkey said, "Since it's a World of Oblivion separated from us by a World of the Future, who knows that he's in the World of Oblivion?"

Hsiang Yü said, "Beautiful Lady, you don't understand. In a place called Fish-mist Village stands the Jade Gate with two doors. Inside the gate is a hidden path that leads to the World of the Future. In the World of the Future there is another hidden path that leads to the World of Oblivion.

"Some time ago there was a man called New Being, also known as Newly Retired Scholar. He was really brave! One day he pushed open the Jade Gate and went to the World of Oblivion, found his father, and returned home. When he came back his hair and beard were completely white. After one visit, that Newly Retired Scholar shouldn't have made a second one, but he wasn't satisfied. So three years later he again went through the Jade Gate, this time to look for his father-in-law. Great Yü, the Dark Emperor, was furious. He didn't wait for him to return, but ordered someone to put seals on the Jade Gate. When the Newly Retired Scholar came back from the World of Oblivion, and found the Jade Gate sealed, he shouted the whole day, but no one answered.

"To the east no one received him, to the west no one cared about him. It's hard to be a man in the middle. Happily, the Newly Retired Scholar was good-natured. He's lived in the World of the Future for more than ten years now and still hasn't come home."

Monkey exclaimed, "Your Majesty, this Jade Gate is truly a wonder. I want to go see it tomorrow!"

King Hsiang said, "That's no trouble. It's only a few steps from here to Fish-mist Village."

As he was speaking, they heard the cock crow three times. Eight green silk windows turned fish-belly white as the sun slowly rose above the eastern mountains—the dawn was exhilarating. Four of Beautiful Lady Yü's maids were walking outside the window. Footsteps could be heard but no voices. Monkey yelled, "P'ing-hsiang! I want to get up."

A maid answered from outside the window, "I'll send her in." Shortly, P'ing-hsiang pushed the door and entered the room. Hsiang Yü helped Monkey up, and they sat together. Another maid rushed in and asked, "Would Your Ladyship come to Heaven's Song Cottage to wash?"

Monkey was about to move when he had another thought and said to himself, "If I'm too hasty, I'll lose Beautiful Lady's grace." He gently pushed open the two panels of a green silk window and picked a pomegranate flower and leaf. He fondled it in his hand, then dropped it to the mosaic pavement.

Monkey turned and left, and not long afterward came to Heaven's Song Cottage. There he saw a silver lacquer box and a box of fragrant powder on a long, exquisitely carved desk. Beside the boxes sat a jade-green crystal cup holding a peach powder puff. To the left of the silver lacquer box was a basin painted with purple flowers, in which there was a hairband. A delicate vase contained dark eyebrow paint. On the right side lay a large comb for oiling the hair and three small ones. On the left lay a set of green jade combs: five medium green jade oil combs, and five small ones. Below them were four large striped rhinoceros horn combs and four small red-stone combs. Above right was placed a delicate ice-jade bottle holding hundred-fragrance cologne. There was also a hundred-nippled cloud-striped jar nearly two-thirds full of alcohol for moistening the fingernails. A stone basin shaped like a square jade seal was placed above left. The basin contained clear water over several curious stones, and across the stones lay a little bamboo bristle brush. Below on the right lay four large and ten small dark and soft brushes and six human-hair brushes. Beside these last brushes lay a half-water and half-oil comb, and two combs with blunt teeth. A pair of gold tweezers, jade-inlaid scissors, a face-cleaning blade, a glass of pure rose-dew, a goblet of green rice-powder for washing hands, and a glass of jade-green fragrant oil were arranged beside an ancient bronze mirror.

When Monkey saw the mirror he quickly took a look to compare himself with the real Beautiful Lady, and saw that the face in the mirror was prettier. Several maids hovered around Monkey: some fixed his hair, some changed his clothes.

When the morning toilet was completed, Hsiang Yü bounded into the lodge and shouted, "Beautiful Lady! Let's go to the Jade Gate!"

Monkey was delighted. Hsiang Yü called for the sedan chair. Monkey said, "You're such a bore, Your Majesty! It's only a short walk in the shade of pines and cedars. It would be so vulgar to take a sedan chair."

Hsiang Yü bellowed, "Forget the sedan chair!"

The two of them went out hand-in-hand and before long arrived at the gate. There were no seals to be seen on it and Monkey pushed it halfway open. He thought, "If I don't go now, when will I?" And he lunged through.

Hsiang Yü was dumbfounded. He sputtered helplessly and grasped at Monkey's skirt, but caught only the air and toppled forward with a thud. Monkey paid him no mind, and went on by himself.

After plunging headlong through the gate, Monkey rolled on and on for several miles. In his ears he heard the cries of the King of Ch'u and the wailing of the maids. After rolling a few more miles, he could no longer hear them, but he still hadn't come to the World of the Future. Monkey grew anxious and shouted, "Oh no! No! All along I've been fooling other people, but now it's me who's been tricked into this bottomless well by Hsiang Yü!"

Suddenly he heard a voice beside him say, "Great Sage, don't worry. You've already come better than half way. It's only a little farther to the World of the Future."

Monkey said, "Big brother, where are you?"

The voice said, "I'm right next door to you, Great Sage."

Monkey said, "Then why don't you open the door and let me come in for tea?"

The voice said, "This is No-man's World. There's no tea to drink."

Monkey said, "If it's No-man's, who's that talking about No-man?"

The voice said, "Great Sage, you're so intelligent—why so dense now? I'm disembodied; in fact, I've never even been joined with a body."

When Monkey saw that no door would be opened, he grew so angry that he put all his strength into rolling, and rolled all the way down to the World of the Future. He had just stood up and taken a few steps when he encountered the Six Thieves he had first met years ago.[6] He snorted and said, "Bah! Time is out of joint—I'm seeing ghosts in broad daylight."

The Six Thieves yelled, "Don't run away, pretty lady. Wait 'til we strip off your clothes and take your jewels to pay for your safe conduct."

---

[6] In chapter 14 of *Journey to the West* Monkey dispatched the Six Thieves, who were threatening to rob his master. The thieves are allegorical representations of delusion resulting from attachment to the six forms of consciousness recognized by Buddhism: sight, hearing, smell, taste, feeling, and thought.

CHAPTER EIGHT

In the World of the Future, Monkey Exterminates the Six Thieves;
As Yama,[1] for Half a Day Monkey Judges Good and Evil.

As Monkey, in the person of Beautiful Lady Yü, plunged helter-skelter through the Jade Gate, he was concentrating on reaching the World of the Future and hadn't returned to his own form. When he heard the threats of the Six Thieves, he realized this and quickly stroked his face to effect the transformation. "Take a good look at my cudgel, you thieves!" he growled.

The courage of the Six Thieves was immediately shattered. They knelt by the side of the road and wailed to Monkey for pity, "Great Sage, Bodhisattva of Mercy, we shouldn't have molested your Master that time under the ivy-covered tree and brought down your noble wrath. We six brothers all lay dead at once. When our spirits went into the World of the Ancients, because of our reputations as thieves, we couldn't stay there. We could only come here and rob in broad daylight to make a living. We haven't done anything even half bad. We kowtow to you, and hope that you'll spare us."

Monkey said, "I could spare you, but you wouldn't have spared me." And he brought down his cudgel and pounded the thieves into meat cakes. Then he walked away, intent on finding the hidden path.

All at once a pair of boys wearing black grabbed Monkey and said, "You've come just in time, my lord Great Sage. Our King Yama took ill and died. The Jade Emperor is busy with some kind of construction work and didn't have time to send anyone—he doesn't care that the Underworld has no master. If my lord Great Sage could take charge for us for only half a day, we would be most grateful."

Monkey thought it out. "If I waste half a day I won't be able to see the First Emperor of Ch'in until tomorrow morning. If the Master

---

[1] Yama is the King of Hell in Buddhist legend.

should be killed by some monster what would I do? What could I do? I'd better send them away."

And he said, "I can do many other things, but I certainly can't be a King Yama. Although I'm a very straightforward person, I can be quick-tempered at times and hurt people. If there were a charge brought to the court of the Underworld and the plaintiff turned out to be right, I might suddenly become angry and take out my cudgel and beat the defendant to pieces. In a case that wasn't clear-cut, it would be all right if there were a firm witness. But if a witness knelt forward and said, 'The plaintiff isn't quite right, and the defendant is so pitiful,' then what would I do?"

The boys wearing black said, "You're mistaken, Great Sage. The question of life and death would be in your hands. What's there to be afraid of?" Disregarding Monkey's protests, they dragged him through the Gate of Ghosts, and called out, "Let all palaces empty to welcome the true King Yama we have found!"

Monkey had no choice but to ascend the main hall. An attendant bailiff presented Monkey with the jade seal and asked him to take charge. At the foot of the stairs stood red-haired devils, green-toothed devils, and a motley group of masterless, homeless devils, numbering in all eighty million four thousand and six hundred. In the front of the hall stood seven-foot-tall bailiffs, tattooed bailiffs, chief-circuit bailiffs, fate-arbiter bailiffs, sun bailiffs, moon bailiffs, lotus bailiffs, water bailiffs, iron-faced bailiffs, white-faced bailiffs, life-suspending bailiffs, sudden-death bailiffs, treachery-penetrating bailiffs, bailiffs who help people onto the correct way, and women bailiffs, in all five million sixteen people. They presented a ledger that listed their names and saluted with, "A thousand years!" Denizens of the nine other Halls of Hell also came to pay their respects.

Monkey sent all of them from the hall. Then Bailiff Ts'ao, responsible for the Life and Death Register, knelt at the foot of the stairs and sent up the register. Monkey took it and leafed through the pages, thinking, "The other day I killed a lot of boys and girls. I wonder if they're listed here?" He turned a page and thought, "If it says that Sun Wu-k'ung beat to death several thousand boys and girls, should I cover it up or must I send a summons?"

He hadn't yet decided when it occurred to him, "Oh, that's right—when I came here before, I just crossed out the names of everyone named Sun,[2] and all those little monkeys still depend on my influence to

---

[2] In chapter 3 of *Journey to the West*, Monkey crossed his own name and those of all simians from the Underworld register, thereby giving them immortality.

keep them free from the judgment of merit and demerit. Anyway, what little devil would dare report what I do? And what little bailiff would dare write it down?"

He flipped over the pages and threw the book down the stairs. Bailiff Ts'ao held it as before and stood beside the left pillar.

Monkey shouted, "Bailiff Ts'ao! Bring me a novel to help me pass the time!"

The bailiff said, "Your Honor, we're extremely busy here. You haven't time to read a novel." He presented a calendar with a yellow binding and said, "Your Honor, your predecessor always followed a calendar."

Monkey opened the calendar and looked it over. Right at the beginning there was the twelfth month and the first month came at the very end. Each month began with the thirtieth or twenty-ninth and ended with the first. Monkey was startled and said, "How strange! In the World of the Future the calendar runs backwards. I can't figure it out!"

He was about to summon the calendar-maker and ask him about it when a bailiff entered the hall and said, "Your Honor, tonight at court we must interrogate the Sung prime minister Ch'in Kuei."[3]

Monkey thought, "This Ch'in Kuei must have been an evil man. If he sees me looking like a compassionate monk, why should he be afraid?" He told the bailiffs "Bring the judicial robes," and he put on the nine-tasseled mortarboard, the robe embroidered with scaly dragons and a pair of iron emotion-repelling shoes. A tin ink-well containing vermilion ink and a copper brush-stand against which leaned two bright red brushes were placed on the table. On the left were arranged a bamboo tube holding slips on which were written the names of minor Underworld clerks, a tube containing slips with the names of all circuit bailiffs, one with the names of bailiffs presiding over courts, and three enumerating the nameless attending devils.

Monkey summoned five kinds of devil-bailiffs. First came the green-robed bailiff leading five hundred green-faced, green-skinned, green-toothed, green-fingered, green-haired devils known as "crack Ch'in-hacking devils." Then came the yellow-turbaned bailiff leading five hundred gold-faced, gold-armored, gold-armed, gold-headed, gold-eyed, gold-toothed "fierce Ch'in-extinguishing devils." The red-bearded bailiff

---

[3] Ch'in Kuei (1090–1155) was prime minister to the first emperor of the Southern Sung dynasty, Kao-tsung. In pursuing a policy of appeasement with the Jurchen Chin dynasty (1115–1234) which had seized northern China, Ch'in Kuei deemed it necessary to eliminate the capable general Yüeh Fei. This act fatally undermined that faction which, inspired by Yüeh Fei's victories, hoped to retake the north, and paved the way for successful peace negotiations.

led five hundred crimson-faced, crimson-bodied, crimson-clothed, crimson-boned, crimson-biled, crimson-hearted "crack Ch'in-shaming devils." The white-bellied bailiff led five hundred white-livered, white-lunged, white-eyed, white-bowelled, white-bodied, white-mouthed "small Ch'in-killing devils." And finally came the dark-faced bailiff leading five hundred black-clothed, black-skirted, black-boned, black-headed, black-footed (in fact only their hearts weren't black) devils called "good Ch'in-flogging devils." The devil brigades corresponded to the five colors, and, in accord with the five phases,[4] they stood in the five directions. They stood in five orderly groups before the Court of Fearful Ambition.

Monkey also called for patrolling messengers, who wore snow-white turbans and had protruding bones and sinews and black faces with coppery eyes, to guard the area beyond the screen on the east side of the hall. Another squad of patrolling messengers wearing blood-spotted turbans and having protruding bones and sinews, powder-colored faces and trunks like elephants guarded the area beyond the western screen. Monkey placed a certain Bailiff Hsü in charge of these messengers.

Then he summoned a unit of six hundred grassy-haired, tattoo-faced, insect-throated, windy-eyed, iron-handed, copper-headed marshals and put Bailiff Ts'ui in charge of them. One hundred dragon-colored devils, wearing fish clothes and having the heads and mouths of tigers and the horns and hooves of cattle, carried letters and official documents. Some male shamans wearing onion-flower hats received guests and saw them off. Two hundred devils with weedy hair rolled up the screens and swept the grounds. Also at hand there were seven hundred musicians, each with nine dragon-feet and the head of a phoenix.

Monkey ordered, "Little devils, raise the iron-wind flagpole." The bailiffs passed on his command and everyone outside the screens assented in one voice. The iron pole was raised to the thundering cadence of three hundred and thirty-three drumbeats. Two great white banners flashed and showed eight characters clearly written in pure gold: "Revenge Evil, Purify Hatred, Honor the Upright, Exterminate Deviants."

Monkey watched as the flagpole was raised and had a notice issued saying:

> From Sun, presiding in the main hall: The way of Heaven is vast; the law is beyond all emotion. A bailiff who adjudicates good and evil must be beyond

---

[4] The five phases of Chinese cosmology are wood, fire, metal, water, and earth, and the directions to which they correspond are east, south, west, north, and the center.

selfishness. Whoever transgresses the law draws himself into its inexorable net. Proclaimed in this third month.

After the notice was displayed, those outside the screens shouted in unison and beat the drum another round. Monkey issued a summons tablet that read: "Ch'in Kuei."

A bailiff knelt, received the tablet, and flew past the screen. When he hung it on the eastern pillar, there was a great commotion beyond the screen and another thundering drum round was sounded. Monkey shouted, "Roll up the screens!" Several devils rushed in and rolled up the fighting-tiger screens. All the bailiffs stood facing each other from either side of the hall in flying-goose formation and glared like eagles. From outside there came another round of drumbeats. A conch-shell was blown and cloud chimes struck. A white paper banner was brought in to the chaotic clatter of stones, and on it was written: "The Sung thief, Ch'in Kuei." The devil-attendants at the first gate shouted, "Bring in the Sung thief, Ch'in Kuei!"

Assent came in unison from outside the screen and the drum again thundered. The conch was again blown and the cloud chimes struck. In the hall a green-toothed bailiff began to sound the Deviant-eliminating Bell. There were drum rolls from the outer gate, drum rolls from the inner gate, and drum rolls from beyond the screen. Smoke billowed and the stars of the Dipper were scattered.

The devils at the outer gate shouted, "Ch'in Kuei enters!" The five classes of devil bailiffs within the screen and all the devil attendants beyond the screen roared in one voice; the noise was thunderous. When the drumming ceased, Monkey gave the command, "Loosen Ch'in Kuei's bonds! Let me question him carefully."

A thousand jobless devils of heroic spirit quickly released the ropes, dragged Ch'in Kuei down from the stone slab to which he was tied, and kicked him a few times. Ch'in Kuei crouched on the ground, not daring to make a sound.

Monkey called out, "Welcome, Prime Minister Ch'in."

CHAPTER NINE

How Ch'in Kuei, Even with a Hundred Bodies, Could Not Redeem Himself; The Great Sage Wholeheartedly Takes Refuge in Yüeh Fei.

The bailiff in charge of the register again presented his book of merits and demerits. Monkey looked through it and said, "Bailiff, why doesn't the name Ch'in Kuei appear in the record?"

The bailiff answered, "Your Honor, Ch'in Kuei's guilt is great, his evil monstrous. I didn't dare to mix him in with the other ghosts, so I prepared a special record on him and inserted it at the back."

Monkey flipped back the pages and took out the record of Ch'in Kuei's evils. At the beginning it read:

> The ruler of Chin, Wu-ch'i-mai, gave Ch'in Kuei to his brother Ta-lan as a hostage. When Ta-lan attacked Shan-yang, Ch'in Kuei advocated negotiations. Ta-lan thereupon released Ch'in to return home. He was accompanied by his wife née Wang.

Monkey said, "Ch'in Kuei, after you became a minister to your emperor, you didn't seek to elevate yourself or spread your fame. Why did you enter into collusion with Chin?"

Ch'in Kuei said, "This is nothing but the slander of the Chin people. It doesn't have a thing to do with me." Monkey asked a silver-faced, jade-toothed bailiff to bring a treachery-reflecting water mirror. In the mirror Ch'in Kuei was plainly seen prostrate before the Chin king saying, "Ten thousand years." The Chin king whispered in Kuei's ear, and Kuei nodded his head. Ch'in Kuei whispered into the king's ear, and the king smiled. When Ch'in Kuei was about to leave, the Chin king again whispered in his ear, and Ch'in Kuei responded, "It goes without saying! Indeed."

Monkey was enraged. He said, "Ch'in Kuei, do you see the Ch'in Kuei in the mirror?"

Ch'in Kuei said, "But Your Honor, the Ch'in Kuei in the mirror doesn't know the suffering of the one outside the mirror."

Monkey said, "Soon he will know suffering." He ordered iron-faced devils to inflict the "body covered with brambles" punishment. One hundred and fifty devils assented immediately and produced six million embroidery needles, pushing them everywhere into Ch'in Kuei's body. Monkey continued reading:

> In the first year of the Shao-hsing reign (1131), he was appointed vice-civil councilor of state. Kuei concealed his malicious intent, waiting only to attain the prime minister's office.

Monkey threw back his head and roared with laughter. He said, "What were you waiting to do with the prime minister's office?"

Chief Bailiff Kao said, "Today there are two kinds of people who wait for the prime ministership. One kind, the malodorous, who only know how to eat and wear clothes and play with their wives and children, wait until they get the prime ministership and use it to make themselves elegant, to impress people in their home town, and to enslave and cheat others. The second is the kind who sells his country and topples the court, secretly wearing the emperor's mortarboard crown and handing down proclamations under the royal seal. He waits until he gets the prime ministership and uses it to monopolize political power, to control the emperor, and to reward or punish as he wills. Ch'in Kuei was the latter sort."

Monkey ordered small devils to slap Ch'in Kuei's face. A group of red-hearted, red-haired devils all grabbed hold of Ch'in and beat him from nine in the morning till one in the afternoon. Even then they did not want to stop. Monkey shouted, "You red-hearted devils, that's enough! There'll be time for more beating later." He read on:

> In the eighth month he was appointed vice director of state affairs. In the ninth month Lü I-hao again became prime minister; he and Ch'in Kuei shared power. Kuei berated Lü's faction. Promoting internal strength and nonresistance in external affairs, he banished I-hao to Chen-chiang. The emperor told Academician Ch'i Ch'ung-li, "Kuei wants to hand the people of Hopei over to Chin, and the people of the Central Plain to Liu Yü. If Southerners thus return to the South and Northerners to the North and I am a Northerner—where shall I go?

Monkey said, "The Sung emperor was right. In times like this, when common folk in the mountains and valleys receive their draft notices one day and see the imperial announcement the next, which of them doesn't have a loyal heart? And you—to whom did you owe your noble rank among the Three Dukes, your ten-thousand-picul emolument, your official seal with its bright ribbons and your six-willow gate?[1] To whom do you owe your huge courtyard and fancy embroidery? You never thought about your emperor or repaying your country's kindness, but all the time nurtured treachery and poison. You put the emperor, high as the ninth heaven, in a position where he couldn't protect one foot of the crossbeam in his house. Do you call this loyalty? Or treachery!"

Ch'in Kuei answered, "Although I am stupid, I tried to protect the emperor and pacify the realm. 'Southerners return south, and Northerners return north' was nothing but a current joke at the time! Your Honor, you shouldn't take it into account."

Monkey said, "This is no joke!" He ordered the "little dagger-mountain" brought in. Two fierce weedy-haired devils brought out a hill-shaped device bristling with knife blades. They threw Ch'in onto it, and his body dripped with blood.

Monkey said, "This is just for fun, Prime Minister Ch'in. You shouldn't take it into account." And he laughed loudly. He again read:

During the eighth year (1138) he was appointed vice director of state affairs. An envoy of Chin came to negotiate peace with Wang Lun. Kuei went with the prime minister to see the emperor. Kuei alone lingered and said, "Bureaucrats are afraid of this and that. They are of no help in deciding an important matter. If Your Majesty decides to negotiate peace, I beg you to consult with me." The emperor said, "I'll give authority to you alone." Kuei said, "I hope Your Majesty will consider it for three more days."

Monkey said, "Let me ask you—if you wanted to be successful in the negotiations, a matter as urgent as wind and fire, why did you want to wait three days? If there had been an official who was willing to spit blood and swear an oath to form a party of loyalists willing to sacrifice their lives, your plans would have been destroyed."

Ch'in Kuei said, "Your Honor, at that time there was only Emperor Ch'in Kuei. How could there have been an Emperor Chao?[2] This

---

[1] The seal and prescribed number of trees planted at one's gate are indications of rank.
[2] Chao was the surname of the Sung emperors.

ghostly prisoner of yours had a list of court officials that I always kept in my sleeve. If any pro-Chao official should be disrespectful and oppose me, his head would immediately disappear. Tell me, Your Honor, from the time P'an-ku created the world until it returns to Hun-tun, how many such loyalists, willing to sacrifice their lives, might there be? Even if there had been a loyalist at court then, was he going to form a party all by himself? Since no party was formed, I enjoyed peace and luxury."

Monkey said, "Since it was like that, how did the Sung emperor's palace look to you?"

Ch'in Kuei said, "In the eyes of your ghostly prisoner, that day the hundred officials in the palace were all ants."

Monkey ordered, "White-faced devils! Pound Ch'in Kuei into fine powder and change him into a million ants to avenge the grievance of those court officials."

A hundred white-faced devils looked sharp on receiving their command. In a flash they had brought out a pestle fifty feet long and one hundred feet wide and proceeded to crush Ch'in Kuei into a peach-blossom-pink paste. As it spread on the ground, the paste transformed into tiny ants, scurrying hither and thither. Monkey ordered King Puffer's bailiff to come and blow Ch'in Kuei back together again. He asked Ch'in Kuei, "Well, are those hundred officials ants? Or is the prime minister an ant?"

The skin on Ch'in Kuei's face was like dirt. He only sighed. Monkey said, "Now you tell me, Ch'in Kuei, how did the emperor look to you that day?"

Ch'in replied, "When your ghostly prisoner stood in the ranks at court, I looked at the silk five-clawed dragon robe as if it were some old rag in my trunk. I looked at the mortarboard crown as if it were my frayed square cap. I saw the sun-moon fan as if it were my banana leaf, the gold imperial palace as if it were my study. I looked at the gate to the Forbidden City as if it were my bedroom door. As for His Majesty, I saw only a grass-green dragonfly dancing in a circle."

Monkey said, "Enough! I'll trouble you to become an emperor." He ordered the Barons of Light and Dark from the Board of Baleful Heaven to wash Ch'in Kuei in the Sea of Boiling Oil. They tore open his ribs and made them into four wings, changing him into a dragonfly.

Monkey again ordered him blown back to his original form and asked, "Ch'in Kuei, may I further ask how you passed those three days of leisure?"

Ch'in Kuei replied, "How could Ch'in Kuei have any spare time?"

Monkey said, "You are a traitor and a thief. You didn't have to kill barbarians in the West or beat back the Northern Tribes. You didn't have to establish constant principles or rectify names—why didn't you have any spare time?"

Ch'in Kuei said, "Your Honor, during those three days I was busy watching the officials. When I saw one with a heart that had the name 'Ch'in' written on it, I put a vermilion dot above his name. Large dots meant a heart on which 'Ch'in' was large; small dots, a heart on which 'Ch'in' was small. Later on I would appoint the large 'Ch'in' hearts to high posts, while the small 'Ch'in' hearts would suffer a slight reversal. Some could have been either pro-Ch'in or pro-Chao. I left their names unmarked since I planned to banish them later.

"If I found anyone who tended to be pro-Chao, I drew a circle by his name in thick ink. A large circle meant his guilt was great; a small circle meant little guilt. Whether an entire household was wiped out or guilt was shared only by wives and children, whether only one's parents' and wives' families were exterminated or everyone within the nine degrees of relationship were cut down, all depended upon my whim."

Monkey was furious. He shouted, "Brother Chang! Brother Teng! Why didn't you strike him down before? You let him remain in the world to carry on like that? All right—though Lord Teng didn't use his thunderbolts, there's still the thunder of Lord Sun."[3] He ordered ten thousand devils who were imitation thunder gods, each carrying an iron whip, to beat Ch'in Kuei till no trace of him remained. Then he again had the bailiff blow him back to his true form and once more read from the record:

Three days passed. Ch'in Kuei lingered and reported to the emperor as before. Though the emperor was beginning to agree, Kuei was afraid he would change his mind, so he said, "I wish Your Majesty would think it over three more days." After three days the emperor decided in favor of the peace negotiations.

Monkey said, "And how did you pass those three days of leisure?"

Ch'in Kuei said, "I had no leisure those three days either. When I went to court and saw that the Sung emperor had decided in favor of

---

[3] Brother Chang and Brother Teng refer to two of the twenty-four thunder gods in traditional popular legend: Chang Chieh and Teng Chung. In Chinese popular belief, the thunder gods are responsible for making clouds and rain, and for putting evil or treacherous people to death with their thunderbolts. Monkey calls them "brothers" here to show his affection and respect for them.

peace negotiations, it was an accomplishment sweet as honey. When I left the court gates, I went directly to have a feast arranged at Copper Bird Tower to celebrate having conquered Sung, bolstered Chin, and secured my own career. I was drunk the whole day, and the next day I held a great feast for the officials with 'Ch'in hearts.' The music of Chin was performed, along with the 'flying-flower saber dance.' We didn't use any Sung things or say so much as half a word about it. I got good and drunk that day, too. The third day I sat alone in my Sweep-away Loyalty Study and laughed heartily all day. By night I was drunk."

Monkey said, "You really had a fancy for wine those three days, didn't you? Well, today I have several cups of good wine to offer you, Mr. Prime Minister." He ordered two hundred drill devils to carry out a vat of human pus and pour it into Ch'in Kuei's mouth.

Monkey threw back his head and roared with laughter. He said, "The first emperor of Sung, T'ai-tsu, suffered to win the empire. Ch'in Kuei gladly gave it away."

Ch'in Kuei said, "I'm not glad about this human pus wine today. Ah, Your Honor, there will be many Ch'in Kueis in the future—even today their number is not small. Why is it only I who must suffer?"

Monkey said, "Who asked you to be the teacher of today's Ch'in Kueis and the model for future ones?" He ordered the crack gold-clawed devils to bring a saw, tie Ch'in Kuei down, and saw him into ten thousand pieces. From the side, King Puffer's bailiff quickly blew him back together. Monkey again read the ledger:

> After peace negotiations were decided upon, Ch'in Kuei had the Chin people in his power and made himself formidable.

Monkey said, "When you had the Chin people in your power, how many hundred catties did they weigh?"

Ch'in Kuei said, "When I had them in my power they were as heavy as an iron Mount T'ai."

Monkey said, "Do you know how many catties Mount T'ai weighs?"

Ch'in Kuei said, "Probably ten million catties."

Monkey said, "Your guess is off—you can weigh it yourself."

He ordered five thousand copper-boned devils to bring out an iron Mount T'ai and press it on Ch'in Kuei's back. Two hours later, they pushed it aside for a look. They saw a flat Ch'in Kuei, changed into flakes of mud. Monkey ordered him blown back together so he could continue the interrogation. He read:

The Sung generals reported victories in every campaign, but Kuei demanded retreat. In the ninth month he ordered the recall of generals from all fronts.

Monkey asked, "Did those generals return on flying horses or did they walk back to court?"

A bailiff reported, "They naturally returned on flying steeds, Your Honor." Monkey ordered the bailiff in charge of transformations to change Ch'in Kuei into a dappled dragon horse. Several hundred fierce devils rode him and beat him. After an hour Monkey ordered him blown back to his original form and went on reading:

One day he managed to get twelve gold imperial tablets ordering the retreat of Yüeh Fei. After Fei returned, all the territory he had recovered was soon lost again. Fei repeatedly requested to be put in command of the army but was refused. The Chin general Wu-chu sent Kuei a letter and he agreed to its contents. Because Grand Master of Remonstrance Mo-ch'i Hsieh bore a grudge against Fei, Ch'in Kuei goaded Hsieh into impeaching him. Ch'in further instructed Chang Chün to impeach Wang Kuei and lured Wang Chün into bringing false charges against Chang Hsien, saying that the latter plotted for the recall of Fei's army. Kuei ordered a messenger to arrest Yüeh Fei and his son as witnesses against Chang Hsien.

Ch'in Kuei ordered Ho Chu to interrogate Yüeh Fei. Fei's robe at one moment fell open, showing the words "perfect loyalty to repay one's country" etched deep into the skin of his back. Ho Chu saw no evidence to support the charge and declared him innocent.

Ch'in Kuei then shifted the commission to Mo-ch'i Hsieh. After Hsieh had held the office for a little over a month, Yüeh Fei was sentenced to prison. Thus, due to many false testimonies, Yüeh Fei was executed. He was thirty-nine at that time.

Monkey called out, "Ch'in Kuei, how did you feel about General Yüeh's case?" He hardly finished speaking when he saw a hundred Ch'in Kueis prostrate at the foot of the steps, wailing and weeping. Monkey shouted, "Ch'in Kuei, one body is enough for you. Where would the house of Sung get a hundred empires?"

Ch'in Kuei said, "Your Honor, the other things were all right. But when you bring up the case of Lord Yüeh, your ghostly prisoner hasn't enough skin to bear the punishment. If I'm asked about it, I won't have enough words with which to answer. I'm afraid a hundred bodies are too few."

Monkey ordered each bailiff from all the lower courts to take away one Ch'in Kuei and interrogate and torture him. At once ninety-nine

Prime Minister Ch'ins were dispersed to various places. From this side came the cry, "The case of Lord Yüeh has nothing to do with me!" From that side came, "Your Honor, be good. Spare your ghostly prisoner one stroke."

Monkey was pleased. He turned to the bailiffs before his bench and remarked dryly, "I suppose that no criminal law was applied to this case here before?"

Bailiff Ts'ao didn't dare reply, but presented a number of documents for Monkey to look through. He opened them and found they were files from the lower courts of the Underworld. On the first sheet was written:

> Court of Yen: Ch'in Kuei had the nature of "Blue Flies."[4] He plotted the execution of a whole family. Yüeh Fei had moral principles white as snow and enhanced the brilliance of the Yellow Banner.[5] Kuei should be called "stupid thief," and Fei, "perfect patriot."

Monkey said, "This is too lenient. The word 'stupid' is not adequate for Ch'in Kuei."

The second file read:

> Court of Li: Ch'in Kuei's accusation reached an impasse; the "Sorrow of Ch'u" makes one sad.[6]

Monkey said, "This is ridiculous! The crimes of the thief Ch'in are beyond counting and this bailiff takes the time to polish his lines. That proves that 'literary men have difficulty judging a case.' No need to finish it." And he opened the third file:

> Court of T'ang: An Elegy to General Yüeh
>
> *Who issued the three-word condemnation[7]*
> *That shattered this Great Wall of ten thousand miles?*
> *Gaze northward: True, 'tis worthy of tears;*
> *On southern branches, in vain the magpies linger.*

---

[4] "Blue Flies" is the title of an ode in the *Shih Ching* (*Book of Songs*) which admonishes a sovereign not to heed the slanderers who would undermine the nation.

[5] The Yellow Banner is the imperial insignia.

[6] I.e., the song "Li Sao" by Ch'ü Yüan (4th century B.C.).

[7] When it was suggested to Ch'in Kuei that the case against Yüeh Fei was unjust, he replied, "There is no need for proof" (*mo hsü you*)—an expression that became known as "the three-word condemnation."

The country followed him in destruction:
Prime minister and enemies rose at once.
As the sun sets, the pine-wind rises;
Still heard, the clash of sword and spear.

Monkey said, "Here's a poem that cuts through iron and nails." And he called out, "Ch'in Kuei, in Lord T'ang's poem the five-character line 'Prime minister and enemies arose at once' can be called a 'five-word condemnation.' How would it be if I make it match your 'three-word condemnation'? Just now, however, I don't care about your 'three-word condemnation,' nor will I use Lord T'ang's 'five-word condemnation.' I myself have a one-word condemnation."

A bailiff said, "What is the one-word condemnation, Your Honor?"

Monkey said, "Hack!" He immediately ordered a hundred weedy-haired devils to bring out a furnace and forge twelve golden tablets. Outside the screen the drum was beaten three hundred and thirty-three strokes. Countless green-faced long-fanged devils charged in and grabbed hold of Ch'in Kuei. First they hacked him into sections like fish scales, then cut them off piece by piece and threw them in the furnace.

When the fish-scale chopping was finished, Monkey shouted, "Principal Bailiff of Orthodox Records, destroy the first gold tablet!"

Having done this, the bailiff reported in a loud voice, "Your Honor, the first gold tablet ordering the recall of General Yüeh has been destroyed!"

The drum was beaten another thunderous round. From the left fierce red-bodied devils jumped out, each carrying a knife with which to hack Ch'in Kuei. The slices they made looked like lines in ice.

Monkey again shouted, "Principal Bailiff of Orthodox Records, destroy the second gold tablet!"

The bailiff followed the order and reported loudly, "The second gold tablet ordering the recall of General Yüeh is destroyed!"

With another round of drumbeats, ten eyeless, mouthless, blood-faced crimson devils emerged from the east, each carrying a knife with which to hack at Ch'in Kuei. They slashed him into snowflakes.

When the bailiff had destroyed the next tablet he reported, "The third gold tablet ordering the recall of General Yüeh is destroyed." The drum was beaten another round.

Suddenly a drum sounded from the outer gate. A little fish-clothed devil carried in a large red card which he presented to Monkey, who opened it and read it over. Five words were written on the card saying, "Salutations from Sung General Fei." When Bailiff Ts'ao saw this he immediately produced a scroll containing facts about all the officials in history.

Monkey looked through it carefully, and noted the information on Yüeh Fei. The drum was again beaten at the outer gate and gold reed-pipes blew outside the screen. Both were played loudly for an hour. A general strode forward and Monkey quickly descended from the main hall. He bowed with hands clasped, and said, "Welcome, General." After they had climbed the stairs he again bowed deeply with hands clasped. They had just entered within the screens when dear Monkey again did obeisance and said, "Master Yüeh, your disciple has had two masters. The first was the Patriarch Subodhi;[8] the second was the T'ang Priest. Today I have met you, General, my third master, and the Three Teachings[9] are complete within me

General Yüeh demurred repeatedly, but Monkey was insistent. He continued to bow and said, "General Yüeh, today your disciple has a cup of blood wine to set your heart at ease."

General Yüeh said, "Thank you very much, disciple, but I fear I won't be able to drink it."

Then Monkey wrote a letter and looked around, saying "Where are the little devils who carry letters?" A group of ox-headed tiger-horned devils knelt all at once and said, "What is Your Honor's order?"

Monkey said, "I want you to go up to Heaven."

An ox-head replied, "Your Honor, how can a bunch of sunken devils go up to Heaven?"

Monkey said, "It's just that you don't have a way of getting there. Going to Heaven is really no problem." Taking out a piece of paper he changed it into a lucky cloud and gave the letter to the ox-head. Then he remembered, "The day before yesterday the door to Heaven was closed tight. I wonder if it's open today?" He said, "Ox-head, go on this lucky cloud. If you find the door to Heaven closed just say you have a letter from the Underworld for Tushita Palace."[10]

After Monkey had sent the ox-head off, he said, "Master Yüeh, your disciple is most happy. I'll complete a *gāthā* for you."

General Yüeh said, "Disciple, I've spent years on horseback. I've never read a single line of scripture or spoken Ch'an words. How can I give you a *gāthā* to complete?"

Monkey said, "Listen, Master, and I will complete one anyway:

For your ruler, perfect your loyalty;
As an official, repay your country.

---

[8] Subodhi was the master who, in chapter 2 of *Journey to the West*, taught Monkey techniques of longevity and physical transformation.

[9] The Three Teachings are Taoism, as taught Monkey by Subodhi; Buddhism, as taught by the T'ang Priest; and Confucianism, represented by Yüeh Fei.

[10] Tushita Palace is the heavenly residence of Lao-tzu.

Everyone is the King of Heaven;[11]
Everybody is a Buddha.

Monkey had just finished reciting when he saw the ox-headed devil carrying a return letter. Ox-head landed on the stairs with a gold and purple calabash on his head. Monkey asked, "Was the gate of Heaven closed?"

The ox-head replied, "Heaven's gate was wide open."

He presented Lao-tzu's reply. It read:

The Jade Emperor is overjoyed at the Great Sage's interrogation of Ch'in Kuei: every word was true, every beating appropriate. I present you with this gold calabash—avoid using a drill on it! I hope the Great Sage will be careful. As for the business of sky gouging, it's a very long story. I'll tell you about it when we meet.

Monkey read the letter and laughed loudly. He said, "The time I was in Lotus Flower Cave, I shouldn't have drilled open his treasure.[12] Now the old man is being sarcastic." He bowed toward General Yüeh with hands clasped and said, "Please sit a little while, Master, and allow me to prepare the blood wine."

---

[11] Monkey bases the first two lines on the four words Yüeh Fei's mother was believed to have tattooed on her son's back: perfect loyalty to repay one's country.

[12] Monsters Gold Horn and Silver Horn were actually servants of Lao-tzu, sent to earth at the request of Kuan-yin to test the pilgrims. They battled Monkey with several of Lao-tzu's magical devices, among which was a gold and red calabash (*Journey to the West*, chapters 32–35). When anyone at whom the calabash was aimed made a sound indicating the presence of vital energy, he was sucked into it and reduced to pus. Monkey returned the calabash to Lao-tzu after the battle. However, there is no indication in *Journey* that Monkey damaged it.

CHAPTER TEN

Monkey Returns to the Tower of Myriad Mirrors;
In the Palace of Creeping Vines Wu-k'ung Saves Himself.

Monkey took the calabash in his hand and asked a bailiff to stand beside him. He whispered something into the bailiff's ear—we don't know what—and handed him the calabash. The bailiff went to the foot of the stairs, then jumped into the air shouting, "Ch'in Kuei! Ch'in Kuei!"

By then Kuei's heart was dead and his breath alone remained. This gave forth a sound of acknowledgment and was instantaneously sucked into the calabash. Monkey saw this and shouted, "Bring it here! Bring it here!"

The bailiff hurried inside the screen and gave the calabash to Monkey. Monkey pasted a seal reading "Quickly follow the orders of most high Lao-tzu," on the mouth of the calabash. An hour and forty-five minutes later, Ch'in Kuei was transformed into a bloody fluid. Monkey ordered a bailiff to bring out a gold-claw cup. He tipped the calabash and poured out the blood; then, kneeling, he offered the cup with both hands to General Yüeh saying, "Master, drink of Ch'in Kuei's blood wine."

General Yüeh waved it away and wouldn't drink. Monkey said, "Don't be silly, Master Yüeh. You should only hate the thief who stole Sung—you needn't pity him."

General Yüeh said, "I don't pity him."

Monkey said, "If you don't pity him, why not have a mouthful of wine?"

General Yüeh said, "You don't realize, disciple, that if a man on earth were to drink even half a mouthful of that thief and traitor's blood and flesh, his stomach would stink for ten thousand years." Seeing Master Yüeh steadfastly refuse to drink, Monkey called a red-hearted devil and gave it to him. The red-hearted devil drank it and went to the back of the hall.

An hour later there was suddenly a great commotion in front of the gate. The gate-keeper beat the cry-treachery drum. At the foot of the stairs the devils of five colors standing in rank in the five directions and the bailiffs of all courts of the five directions braced for action. Monkey was about to ask a bailiff what was going on when he saw that three hundred weedy-haired devils were already huddled at the foot of the white jade stairs holding the head of a blue-toothed, green-eyed, crimson-haired, red-bearded bailiff. They reported, "Your Honor, as soon as the red-hearted devil drank Ch'in Kuei's blood wine, his face changed. He ran into the Purple Palace of Destiny, pulled a dagger from his belt, and stabbed to death his benevolent master, the Arbiter of Destiny. Then he ran through the Gate of Ghosts and was reincarnated."

Monkey shouted for the devils to go away. Then General Yüeh arose. From beyond the screen came three hundred and thirty-three beats of the drum and gentle strains of music. Lances and blades cracked; swords and spears were thick as a forest. Fifty thousand chief bailiffs kowtowed to send off Lord Yüeh.

Monkey said to them, "Arise and leave us." The chief bailiffs responded to the order and retired to their own courts. Then countless fierce green-blooded, red-muscled devils prostrated themselves to send off Lord Yüeh. Monkey told them, "Arise and leave us."

Three hundred upholding-righteousness yellow-toothed devils raised precious spears and shouted, "Farewell, Lord Yüeh!" Monkey commanded, "Yellow-toothed devils, you will escort Lord Yüeh to his residence!" Monkey and Yüeh Fei walked to the outer gate. Another round of drumbeats was sounded and the music of the gold reed-pipes trilled. Monkey bowed with clasped hands and accompanied General Yüeh to the Gate of Ghosts. The drum thundered another round. Ten thousand devils shouted with one voice and Monkey bowed deeply with hands clasped to see General Yüeh through the gate.

He said loudly, "When you have some free time, Master, I'll come to receive instruction." Bowing with hands clasped once more, he finally saw Master Yüeh off.

Immediately he leapt into the air and threw the mortarboard, the entwining-dragon robe, the pair of iron emotion-repelling shoes, and the square jade seal of King Yama down onto the Gate of Ghosts and left.

★   ★   ★

It is said that in Shantung Province there was a restaurant whose manager had lost all his hair and teeth. No one knew how many hundreds of years old he might be. All day long he sat in his shop and sold food. His sign said, "This is the Restaurant of the New Ancient." Beneath this a line of small characters read, "Original name: Newly Retired Scholar."

When the Newly Retired Scholar returned from the World of Oblivion, he had found the Jade Gate tightly closed and couldn't pass through to the World of the Ancients. Consequently, he stayed in the World of the Future and opened a restaurant to pass his days. But he was a man unwilling to forget his roots, so he changed his name to the New Ancient.

That particular day he was sitting in his shop drinking tea when he saw Monkey running heavily from the east, shouting, "What a stench! What a terrible stench!"

The New Ancient said, "Good day, Sir."

Monkey stopped. "And who are you that you dare to call me 'Sir'?"

The New Ancient said, "I'm an ancient contemporary and a contemporary ancient. If I told you who I am you'd just laugh at me."

Monkey said, "Go ahead and tell me, I won't laugh."

The New Ancient said, "I'm the Newly Retired Scholar, who used to live in the World of the Ancients."

When he heard this, Monkey made a quick salute with clasped hands and said, "My new benefactor! If it hadn't been for your help, I'd have had a hard time getting through the Jade Gate."

The New Ancient was startled, so Monkey told him his name and recounted the whole story. The New Ancient laughed and said, "Well, Mr. Sun, you still owe me a kowtow then."

Monkey said, "Don't joke about it. I have something important to ask you. What's causing this stench? It's not quite dead fish; then again it's not the smell of sheep, either."

The New Ancient said, "If you want rankness, this is the place to come; if not, stay away. We're right next to the Tartars here. If you walk around for a while, your whole body will become rank, too."

When Monkey heard this, he thought, "I'm covered all over with hair. If I become polluted with this smell, I'll be a rank ape. What's more, I was just King Yama and interrogated a certain Ch'in Kuei into one thousand bits and ten thousand pieces. Come to think of it, the First Emperor of Ch'in was a Ch'in, and Ch'in Kuei was a Ch'in. If Kuei wasn't his descendant, he was surely of the same clan—so the First Emperor will surely hold a grudge against me, and won't easily let go of the Mountain-removing Bell. If I were to get rough and steal it, I'm afraid I'd ruin my reputation. Better to ask the Newly Retired Scholar a question, then leap out of this mirror." He said, "New Benefactor, do you know how I can get to the Emerald Green World?"

The New Ancient said, "The way you came is the way to go."

Monkey said, "What slippery Ch'an talk! I know the way I came— rolling from the World of the Ancients down to the World of the Future was easy. But rolling up from the World of the Future to the World of the Ancients will be tough."

The New Ancient said, "If that's your problem, follow me. Come on!" He took Monkey with one hand and dragged him along until they came to a pool of blue water. Without uttering a word the New Ancient pushed Monkey and splash! he fell right back into the Tower of Myriad Mirrors.

Monkey looked around wondering which mirror to leap into. Afraid of wasting time and delaying his master, he turned about, hoping to descend from the tower, but a long search for stairs proved futile. He became anxious and pushed open a pair of sapphire windows. Outside the windows was a maze of exquisite crimson railings arrayed like cracks in ice. Luckily the spaces between supports were rather wide, and Monkey hunched up and scurried through one. Who'd have thought fate was against him, that the time was wrong, or that railings could catch one up? What were clearly railings arranged like cracks in ice suddenly became hundreds of red threads that tangled about Monkey so he couldn't move an inch.

Monkey changed into a pearl and the red threads became a pearl-net. When Monkey couldn't roll through he instantly changed into a blue-bladed sword. The red threads became a scabbard. Monkey had no choice but to return to his own form. He cried, "Master, where are you? Don't you know your disciple is in a lot of trouble?" And his tears fell like water from a spring.

Suddenly there was a flash before his eyes and an old man appeared in the air. Saluting Monkey with his clasped hands he asked, "What are you doing here, Great Sage?"

After Monkey had moaned the reasons, the old man said, "You don't realize that this is the palace of Little Moon King in the Emerald Green World. Once he was a student of mine. Later when he became a king, he spent his days in dissipation. He built thirteen palaces, corresponding to the thirteen classics. This is the Sixty-four Hexagram

Palace.[1] When you became confused, you walked directly into the Palace of Entangling Vines of the hexagram Oppression[2] and were bound tight. I'll loosen the red threads for you and let you go search for your Master."

With tears in his eyes Monkey said, "If you can do this, Elder, I'll never be able to thank you enough."

The old man straightaway snapped the red threads one by one with his hands. Monkey, at last free, bowed very low and asked, "What is your name, Elder? When I see Buddha, I'll register a great merit for you."

The old man said, "Great Sage, I'm called Sun Wu-k'ung."

Monkey said, "I'm called Sun Wu-k'ung, and you're called Sun Wu-k'ung, too. How can one Ledger of Merit have two Sun Wu-k'ungs? Why don't you tell me what you usually do for a living so I can remember a few facts about you?"

The old man said, "You ask me what I do? I'm afraid it's enough to scare a person to death! Five hundred years ago I wanted to seize the Heavenly Palace and situate myself there. The Jade Emperor made me Groom of the Heavenly Stables. Great Sage Equal to Heaven—that's me. I suffered a bit beneath Five Phases Mountain—suffered a bit until the T'ang Priest came. I followed him seeking the 'true fruit.' There was danger and misfortune along the road to the Western Paradise. I chanced upon the Emerald Green World and have been hiding here ever since."

Monkey was furious and said, "You rascally six-eared ape![3] Have you come to trick me again? Take a look at my cudgel!" He pulled his cudgel from his ear and swung it down in front of him.

The old man drew in his sleeves and left. He called back, "This is what is called saving oneself! Too bad you're not real! Not real! . . . Not real! . . . "

A beam of gold light struck Monkey's eyes, and the old man's form vanished. Only then did Monkey realize that the apparition had been his own true spirit. He quickly made a deep bow to thank himself.

---

[1] The Sixty-four Hexagram Palace is named for the *I Ching*. The hexagrams which along with their commentaries comprise the *I Ching* represent the sixty-four permutations of solid and broken lines assembled in figures of six lines each.

[2] This refers to the top line of the *I Ching* hexagram *k'un*, which says, "One is entangled by creeping vines."

[3] In chapters 57 and 58 of *Journey to the West* Monkey confronts a false Monkey, who wants to start his own pilgrimage. The two are so identical that the T'ang Priest, Kuan-yin, the Jade Emperor, Lao-tzu, and the Kings of the Underworld cannot tell them apart. It is Buddha who finally straightens out the matter and identifies the imposter as the Six-eared Monkey.

CHAPTER ELEVEN

Reading Accounts Before the Palace of the Hexagram of Limitation;
Collecting Hairs on the Crest of the Hill of Grief.

When Monkey had finished thanking himself, he jumped down from the tower and walked to a gate. Above the gate hung a stone tablet inscribed with three large characters: "Limitation Hexagram Palace." A purple and gold rope with a limitation hexagram carved from green jade dangling at its end hung from the door-post. The gate had two doors. Water ripples were painted on one and the other was painted with rivers and marshes. On either side of the doors were pasted "spring couplets" written on cloud-swirl paper. The couplets said:

> *Do not leave the gate, do not leave the door:*
> *Danger on earth, danger in heaven.*
> *For the youngest daughter, for mouth and tongue:*
> *Limit sweet, limit bitter.*[1]

After Monkey had finished reading, he made to go right in, but stopped in his tracks and thought, "Since this Emerald Green World has things like red threads that entangle people, I can't go just anywhere. First I'll take a look around this gate and see what I can find out. Then I can look for the old monk."

He turned and walked through the gate's east side-door. Inside, a notice was pasted on a slanting wall. It said:

> Grand Total of Wages for the Carpenters, Masons, and Miscellaneous Workers Who Built Limitation Hexagram Palace:

---

[1] The Limitation (*chieh*) hexagram of the *I Ching* is not an auspicious one, and most of the images in these two couplets are drawn from the explanations of the various lines. The "youngest daughter" and "mouth and tongue" are attributes of the hexagram's top three lines, the trigram *tui*.

Limitation Hexagram Main Palace—sixty-four large and small halls. Carpenters: 16,000 ounces silver. Masons: 18,001 ounces silver. Miscellaneous: 54,060 ounces silver and 7 cash only.

Limitation's Creative Hall[2]—sixty-four chambers. The day before yesterday a sworn brother of Little Moon King, who, though 30 or 40 years of age, had neither been capped[3] nor married, acquired a wife named Lady Green-twine through Little Moon King. The ceremony was held in the third palace. Having been married only one night, they suddenly started a row. Little Moon King was enraged. He ordered me to come in for punishment—fifty strokes of the board. This came about because all the workmen got me into trouble. Just for that I'm cutting their salary to one-sixth. Carpenters only deserve 50,000 ounces silver. Masons only deserve 40,000 ounces silver. Miscellaneous only deserve 200,000 ounces silver.

Limitation's Receptive Hall—sixty-four chambers. Carpenters, masons, and miscellaneous paid as above.

Limitation's Peace Hall—four-hundred and six White Crane Chambers. Little Moon King especially praised the Little Lotus Lodge. Each laborer receives an increase of 500 ounces, which brings the total to: Carpenters: 7,000,000 ounces silver. Masons: 664 ounces silver. Miscellaneous: 2,008,000 ounces silver only.

Limitation's Stagnation Hall (Little Moon King's sleeping quarters) 15,000 Sky-blue Chambers. Little Moon King wanted to add a mirror tower, but recently several additional worlds have emerged: a small one, the World of Current Literature, broke off from the Headache World; a Red Garment World broke off from the World of Wild Herbs; and a Book-burning World broke off from the Lotus Flower World. There are countless other new split-off worlds as well. The oppressive Tower of Myriad Mirrors of the hexagram Oppression cannot contain them all. Therefore, he had no choice but to build a second Tower of Myriad Mirrors here. Tomorrow all workers will come and begin construction. Everyone must be diligent but not overly hasty or he will find himself in trouble. First, however, payment for the last job will be made as follows: Carpenters: 5,005,000 ounces silver. Masons: 40,000,000 ounces silver. Miscellaneous: 1,800,000 ounces silver and 8 cash, 5 and 1/10 cents only.

Monkey read until his eyes grew tired, though a list of sixty other palaces followed after. So adopting a Huai-su[4] method, he took in the rest at a single glance. When he had finished he was afraid and said, "I've seen

---

[2] This palace and the three that follow are named after hexagrams in the *I Ching*.

[3] The "capping" of a young man at twenty years of age ritually symbolized his attainment of maturity.

[4] Huai-su was a very learned disciple of Hsüan-tsang. Legend has it that he was known for his ability to read sūtras at great speed.

the Heavenly Palace and the Isle of P'eng,[5] too. But I've never seen anything like this Sixty-four Hexagram Palace. Now sixty-four hexagrams are not a great number but each hexagram also contains sixty-four palaces. Sixty-four times sixty-four is still a small number, but each of those again has sixty-four palaces. And this place is not the only one—there are twelve more besides. It's hard to imagine seeing it all with my eyes—it's weird enough to be a dream."

He thought of a plan right away. He plucked a handful of hairs from his body, chewed them into tiny pieces, and commanded, "Change!" The hairs became countless little monkeys, who stood huddled together. Monkey barked orders at them: "If you come upon something worth looking at, stop and look it over. Then report to me at once. Don't dawdle!"

The little monkeys ran east, west, south, and north, jumping and dancing. After Monkey sent them off, he went for a leisurely stroll, and came to the crest of the Hill of Grief. He raised his head and saw a little boy carrying a letter.

As the boy walked he grumbled, "Man! You're ridiculous, Boss! What's so special about you that you can cause so many problems? Now I've got to carry another letter to that old official Wang the Fourth. The other day it didn't matter, but this afternoon Mr. Ch'en is drinking and watching a play in our Drinking Rainbow Pavilion, and I won't be able to stick around because of your little matter!"

When Monkey heard that the Master was in Drinking Rainbow Pavilion he wanted to turn around and go looking for him. But he thought better about it and said, "If I just walk to the east or west, I might blunder onto the wrong road. It'd be better to ask that boy." And he said, "Young Master ... "

The boy was walking along, talking to himself, and hadn't raised his head or noticed Monkey. Who would have thought that when he suddenly saw Monkey, blood would flow from the seven apertures of his head. He dropped to the ground unconscious. Monkey laughed and said, "Good boy, you know how to play dead. Let me see about this letter you're carrying."

He quickly took the letter, and when he opened it he saw written on two sheets of coarse yellow paper:

Head Foreman in Charge of the Thirteen Palaces, Shen Ching-nan offers these words for the information of Your Honor, Old Official Wang the Fourth:

---

[5] The Isle of P'eng(-lai) is a mythical island inhabited by immortals.

Though I am worthless, Your Honor has looked with favor upon me and promoted me to head foreman. I didn't know that a thief of thieves had caused Your Honor worry.

Even I wish to cultivate the purity of my worthless name. Hasn't all my behavior for the past several years been virtuous? Yesterday, however, Foreman Yü suddenly reported that items totaling over one hundred have disappeared from the Sixty-four Hexagram Palace, the Palace of Three Hundred Odes, and the Palace of the Eighteen Songs.

His Majesty Little Moon King was very angry. Tomorrow he will commission you, Old Official Wang the Fourth, to inspect and take an inventory of the palaces one by one.

I believe Your Honor is kindhearted. Even if I didn't tell you, you would take care of everything. Yet I still fear my heart won't be clean, but will suffer from this grievance for a hundred years. If your Honor can make a good beginning and end of this matter, I should be grateful for the rest of my life.

I, Shen Ching-nan, your student, attendant to your intimate instructions, and head foreman of thirteen palaces, bow a hundred bows.

To the Old Official, Old Father, Old Master and Lord, Wang the Fourth.

Monkey was determined to find his Master. When he had finished reading he shook his body to call back his hairs. A little monkey came flying up the hill and shouted, "Great Sage! Great Sage! So you've come here! I've been looking for you a long time."

Monkey said, "What have you seen?"

The little monkey said, "I came to a fairy cave where I saw a white deer speaking."

Meanwhile, two little monkeys were fighting their way up the hill, yanking each other's fur and tugging each other's ears. They knelt down together in front of Monkey. One of them said that the other little monkey ate one more double-flowering peach than he had. The other said the first plucked one more plum than he had.

Monkey let out a roar and the three of them jumped back onto his body at once. A while later another group of little monkeys came from the northeast. Some said what they had seen was interesting, some said what they had seen was not. One reported having seen two lines written on a wall:

The mind follows flowing water; it stops at the blue hills.
When I see the fallen flowers are gone, I know that spring has departed.

Another said that an immortal stood on each leaf of a spiraea bush. Each immortal held a pair of fish-shaped castanets and sang loudly to himself:

Return to me the thing-less self,
Return to me the self-less things.
The Void is host;
Things and I are all guests.

One little monkey said, "The clouds in a fairy cave all formed a tapestry of palindromes."

Another little monkey reported, "I saw a high pavilion made of *garu*-wood."

A third said, "There was an ancient fairy cave with its door shut tight. They wouldn't let me in."

A fourth said, "I found a green bamboo fairy cave, but it was very dark and deep and I was scared to go in."

Monkey didn't have the patience to listen. He gave his body a shake and the hundred million monkeys jumped onto his body with the sound "ting-tung, ting-tung." Monkey picked up his feet to walk away, but he heard the hairs on his body say, "Don't go, Great Sage. We have a friend who hasn't returned yet."

Monkey stopped. He saw one last little monkey drunkenly climbing the hill from the southwest. Monkey asked him, "Where did you go?"

The monkey replied, "I was walking close to a tower where there was a girl of just sixteen with a face like peach blossoms. When she saw me outside her window she grabbed me and pulled me in. We sat shoulder-to-shoulder and she poured wine in my mouth till I was drunk as mud."

Monkey was enraged. He clenched his fist in front of the little monkey and beat and scolded him wildly. He said, "You dog! I let you go for a minute and you get tangled up with the Demon of Desire!"

That monkey wailed and wept, and could do nothing but jump onto Monkey's body. Having then gathered all his hairs, Monkey descended the Hill of Grief.

CHAPTER TWELVE

In the Palace of Crying Ospreys,[1] *the Tears of the T'ang Priest Fall;*
A Young Girl Plucks the P'i-p'a[2] *and Sings a Tale.*

Monkey picked up his feet and walked to a tower pavilion that clearly seemed to be the Drinking Rainbow Pavilion. But he didn't see his Master, and his heart became anxious. He turned to look out over an expanse of blue water, in the middle of which stood a water palace. Two men wearing square cloth caps sat in the palace. Monkey was suspicious and quickly scampered up a hill near the tower. He hid in a fold of the hill and looking carefully, spied four elegantly done green characters on the building that read, "Crying Ospreys Water Palace."

The bright walls were colorful as tapestries; the ornamented grounds followed a design. There were cinnamon timbers and orchid rafters, plum-wood beams and orchid chambers. The railings that surrounded the palace were randomly decked with coral. Because they had been there many years, blue-green water weeds had grown around them to make patterns like the spidery characters on an old bronze.

As for the two men in the palace, one wore a nine-flowered *T'ai-hua*[3] cap, and the other man wore a fashionable *Tung-t'ing*[4] cap. The one wearing a nine-flowered cap had a fair complexion, red lips, fine eyebrows, and white teeth. Except for his cap he looked just like the T'ang Priest. Monkey was at once startled and pleased. He thought, "The man in the nine-flowered cap is obviously my Master, but why is he wearing a cap? Little Moon King doesn't *look* like a monster."

---

[1] The Palace of Crying Ospreys is named for the first song in the *Shih Ching*. The song is about a marriage between a gentleman and a fair lady.
[2] The *p'i-p'a* is a four-stringed instrument similar to the lute in appearance.
[3] T'ai-hua is the name of a mountain in Shensi Province.
[4] Tung-t'ing is the name of a lake in Hunan Province.

He was confused, his mind tied in knots. Just as he was about to present himself and drag his Master away, he thought, "Suppose the Master's heart has been turned. There'll be no use in going to the West."

He remained hidden in the fold of the hill, and fixed his eyes for another look, hoping to find out whether this really was his Master. Below he saw the man in the *Tung-t'ing* cap say to the other, "The evening clouds are magnificent. Get up, Mr. Ch'en—we'll take a walk."

The capped T'ang Priest said, "Please, you first, Little Moon King." The two of them walked hand-in-hand to the Pavilion of Dripping Desire. In the pavilion were several scrolls, all of them paintings and calligraphy by famous artists. On the side hung a small scroll with characters written in green:

Green mountains encircle the neck;
A white stream pierces the heart.
Where is the jade lady?
In the empty sky, a white cloud.

The two of them strolled a short way and heard muffled voices from a bamboo grove. The T'ang Priest leaned on a railing and listened. A gust of wind in the pines carried the words of a song:

The crescent moon illumines several regions;
Many families are happy, many are sad.
Some dwell behind jade-tasseled, gold-hooked bed-curtains;
Some float in rainy-night boats on the rivers Hsiao and Hsiang.
Midnight—a girl beats her coverlet;
"Why did you leave me? Why didn't you stay?
If by the third watch tomorrow I haven't seen you,
I'll cut up this quilt embroidered with love birds."

When the T'ang Priest heard this, he nodded his head and his tears fell. Little Moon King said, "I think you've been away from home too long, Mr. Ch'en. Hearing this song has made you sad. Let's go to the Tower that Punctures Blue Heaven to hear a story sung."

The two of them chatted for a while, then left the Pavilion of Dripping Desire and disappeared. Why do you think they disappeared? It happened that the Tower that Punctures Blue Heaven was separated from the Water Palace of Crying Ospreys by a thousand chambers. Everywhere the eye could see trails of flowers encircled the eaves. Green trees arched over crisscrossed paths—a thousand drooping willows and *t'ung* trees a hundred feet tall. The two men made their way along the paths, and, as Monkey sat hidden in the fold of a hill opposite how could he see them?

Two hours later he suddenly made out the same nine-flower-capped T'ang Priest and *Tung-t'ing*-capped Little Moon King sitting across from each other in two armchairs in the tower. Before them was a green striped pot filled with tea and two square Han dynasty-style tea mugs. Three blind girls sat on a low couch. One was called Ko-ch'iang-hua, another Mo-t'an-lang, and the third Pei-chuan-p'ing-t'ing. Though blind, they were very pretty. Each held a *p'i-p'a* pressed against her jade-white breast.

Little Moon King said, "Ko-ch'iang-hua, how many stories can you sing?"

Ko-ch'iang-hua said, "Your Majesty, there was much suffering in the past, but there will be less in the future. There are many, many stories. All that matters is which one Mr. Ch'en would like to hear."

Little Moon King said, "Mr. Ch'en is actually familiar with many stories. Why don't you name the ones you know?"

Ko-ch'iang-hua said, "There's no need to mention the old stories, I'll only name the new ones. There are 'Warm Chats in Jade Hall,' 'The Sad Story of Following the Ways of Heaven,' and 'The Tale of the Western Journey.'"

Little Moon King said, "'The Tale of the Western Journey' is new. That's the one! Sing that one!

The girls agreed. They strummed their *p'i-p'a*s and sang in full voice.

A poem says:
Don't drink while flutes and songs o'erflow the painted hall:
Only in old age can one believe that life is a long dream.
Now I've made a secret compact with my heart,
As I peacefully gaze at a stick of incense in my hushed study.

Ko-ch'iang-hua plucked twenty-seven notes of the sad *p'i-p'a* tune. She sang in a remote and penetrating voice:

The day Heaven's emperor spread out the stars,[5]
Nine constellations and five regions, he set up the cosmos.

---

[5] This song provides a brief, if opaque, summary of Chinese history from the mythical beginning of the universe to the early T'ang period. It shows that all of human history is nothing but amassed desire.

Shooting the sun and pursuing clouds were marks of an earlier era;[6]
Fish-scale clouds, pearl-drop rain arrayed in a hundred forms.
Wu-huai's silver bamboo had many fantastic joints;
King Ko-t'ien's auspicious leaves were congealed fragrance.[7]
Dragon and snake[8]*—mind-pictures handed down on green tablets;*
Crow and rabbit[9]*—signatures inscribed on jade ice.*
Don't mention the mountains' mien or words on stone;
Don't talk about the old men on Sung-feng road.[10]
A jade sank in the Western Sea wrapped in a flowered tapestry.
Upright officials were rewarded in the Palace of Precious Jade.
Hsü Yu fled the emperor's dragon robe,[11]
And the empire was proffered to Lord Yü Shun.[12]
In the fourteenth year, the calamity of bells and stone chimes;
And in time the elder from Tung-t'ing Lake ruled the people.[13]
T'ang the Successful prayed at Mulberry Grove;[14]
Tears sprinkled pearled sleeves on Deer Terrace.[15]

---

[6] Once during the reign of the sage-emperor Yao, ten suns arose, causing great damage to the earth and leaving the people prey to starvation and pestilence. Yao commissioned the archer Hou I to shoot down nine of the suns. Pursuing clouds probably refers to Ch'ang O's flight to the moon. See note 8 in chapter 2.

[7] Wu-huai and Ko-t'ien were kings who ruled over Mt. T'ai at the dawn of time. Silver bamboo has occasionally been used as a metaphor for rain, and auspicious leaves for snow; and if such is the case here, the images might be intended to evoke the harmony with nature that prevailed during those arcadian reigns.

[8] Besides its literal meaning, "dragon and snake" is sometimes used as a figure for men of outstanding talent, and sometimes as a metaphor for twisting, writhing things like cursive-style calligraphy or running water.

[9] Crow and rabbit are usually associated with the sun and moon, respectively.

[10] These are the four immortals of Mt. Sung: Mu Ch'ao-nan, Lin Ta-chieh, Sun Wen-wei, and Shih Mei-ch'iu.

[11] Hsü Yu was a scholar to whom the sage-emperor Yao offered the throne. Hsü refused in favor of a life of reclusion.

[12] Shun, the sage-emperor who succeeded Yao to the throne.

[13] In the fourteenth year of Shun's reign, while the ceremonial playing of bells and stone chimes was in progress, a great storm of wind and rain arose, scattering the musical instruments, destroying houses, and uprooting trees. Shun interpreted this as a sign that no man could hope to rule forever, and he presented Yü the Great, the elder from Tung-t'ing Lake, to Heaven as his successor. Yü did not actually succeed to the throne for another thirty-nine years.

[14] T'ang the Successful seized the throne from the degenerate Chieh, last ruler of the Hsia dynasty, and founded the Shang dynasty. For the first eleven years of his reign a great drought was upon the land, so he sacrificed in the Mulberry Grove and brought rain.

Rain banner and wind axe opened a pure world;
On Kou-ch'en Rampart[16] *King Wu's Chou was founded.*
For the Wu King stones of Spring and Autumn times, lament;[17]
For she who sharpened a clasp in the Warring States, grieve.[18]
White their robes and hats for Yen's champion;
Red in the sky the bold heart of the prince.[19]
"Ting, ting" the dulcimer, mode changed from chih *to* yü;
Flying clouds on River I, ten-thousand layers deep.
Six states died when the plot against Ch'in failed;[20]
Then for the first time "emperor" was carved upon a stone.[21]
Who would have thought there'd be only three Ch'in emperors?
Mermaid candles burned away, the Eastern Sea grew dim.
Sad the lament for the stallion and the beautiful lady;[22]
Having just lifted mountains, he wept in the autumn wind.
The Four White-hairs of firm resolve[23] *sat on the empty mountain;*

---

[15] Deer Terrace was the extravagant terrace built by the wicked Chou, the last ruler of the Shang dynasty. It was there that he perished, arrayed in gem-studded garments, in a fire set by his own hand.

[16] Kou-ch'en Rampart was the place at which the feudal lords rallied under King Wu for the campaign that ended the Shang dynasty and led to the establishment of the Chou.

[17] When Fu-ch'ai, the last king of the Spring and Autumn period state of Wu, wished to attack the state of Ch'i, he was advised by Wu Tzu-hsü to exterminate the state of Yüeh instead. Ch'i, said Tzu-hsü, had not the use of a stony field to Wu as long as Yüeh existed. But Fu-ch'ai ignored the warning, and in time found cause to force Tzu-hsü to commit suicide. Twelve years later, when Wu fell to Yüeh, Fu-ch'ai's last words were, "Would that I had heeded the words of Tzu-hsü."

[18] The wife of King Tai of the Warring States period state of Chao killed herself with a sharpened hair clasp upon learning that her husband had been assassinated.

[19] In 227 B.C., Tan, the crown prince of Yen, recruited Ching K'o to attempt the assassination of the King of Ch'in, later to become the First Emperor of Ch'in. Knowing how slight were the chances of success, the prince and his entourage dressed in white, the color of mourning, when they accompanied Ching K'o as far as River I. There, one of the number played a dulcimer tune in the mournful *pien-chih* mode. Ching K'o sang along and then shifted to the mode of *yü*, stirring all present with the martial feeling of the music.

[20] Ching K'o's attempt at assassination failed, and in a short time Ch'in had defeated the other six states contending for supremacy.

[21] After the conquest of the six states, the King of Ch'in then became the first in Chinese history to take for himself the title of emperor.

[22] The song Hsiang Yü sang for Beautiful Lady Yü and his favorite horse, Dapple, on the eve of his defeat by the Han forces.

[23] Four gray-haired gentlemen known as Master Tung-yüan, Ch'i Li-chi, Master Hsia-huang, and Mr. Lu-li, who fled the tyranny of the Ch'in dynasty to live in seclusion on Mt. Shang.

The tireless Chang Liang kept company with Master Red Pine.[24]
When the spirit of that true man[25] *soared thirty-thousand feet*
The Five Mountains[26] *in unison shouted, "Ten-thousand springs!"*
It is fate that grass should yellow and leaves should fall;
The swords of Tung and Ts'ao[27] *carved up the House of Han.*
Then came a succession of powder-puff emperors—the Six Dynasties[28]*—*
Colored frost and jade dew woven in patterns of ice.
It ended, the pulsing of sixes and nines,[29] *with the choice of an emperor;*
The wise, intelligent T'ang T'ai-tsung was pushed to the fore.
His family affairs were dark, difficult to plumb;
Don't imitate poets who satirize sandflies and centipedes.
Only because in years past beacon fires signaled the alarm by day
Did peach blossoms in the third month shine upon a jade horse.[30]
Before the horse the full moon cast a bow-shaped shadow;
A pair of stars in heaven above entered sword-shaped rainbows.[31]
Soldiers had no heart to grieve for jade and stones;

---

[24] Chang Liang was one of Liu Pang's most trusted advisors. After Liu had established the Han dynasty, Chang Liang turned his attention to the esoteric mysteries of Taoism. Master Red Pine is a Taoist immortal.

[25] I.e., the founder of the Han dynasty, Liu Pang. The ascension of Liu Pang's spirit high up into the sky symbolizes his rise in political career.

[26] The Five Sacred Mountains are Mt. T'ai in the east, Mt. Heng in the south, Mt. Hua in the west, Mt. Heng in the north, and Mt. Sung in the center.

[27] Tung Cho became *de facto* ruler in the chaotic atmosphere of the declining Later Han dynasty and wasted the empire with his cruelty and rapacity. Ts'ao Ts'ao eventually filled the power vacuum left with the assassination of Tung Cho in A.D. 192 and became in turn *de facto* ruler over the empire.

[28] The period in Chinese history between the fall of the house of Wei in A.D. 265, ending the Three Kingdoms period, and the reunification of the empire under the Sui dynasty in A.D. 589.

[29] In Chinese numerology six is the number of the greater yin, and nine, of the greater yang. The pulsing of yin and yang, the two primary cosmic forces, refers to the government instability that marked the Six Dynasties period.

[30] Beacon fires were burned as signals in time of war, and these two lines allude to the turbulence during the transition from the Sui dynasty to the T'ang. In the third lunar month of A.D. 618, Yang-ti, the second emperor of Sui, was assassinated by retainers. At the time "Peach-plum Boys" was a popular reference to the sons of Li (the same character means "pear") family that founded the T'ang dynasty. Jade Horse was a name for one of the carriages in the T'ang imperial procession. Hence, the line might be taken to mean that with the death of Sui Yang-ti the Li family aura was cast over the throne.

[31] In A.D. 626 Li Shih-min (T'ang T'ai-tsung) murdered his brothers Chien-ch'eng, the crown prince, and Yüan-chi at Hsüan-wu Gate. The bow-shaped shadow may portray Shih-min's party awaiting their prey with weapons poised, and the pair of stars of the following line might be the two brothers, who were decapitated after being shot down.

The Dragon's troops paid no heed to anguished souls on the River Hsiang.
In one night, sand- and wind-aggrieved ghosts were entombed;
In mountain valleys year by year were offered tracks of tears.[32]
A voice, a voice spoke only hatred for the emperor of T'ang;
What mattered the lavish newness of your plum blossoms?

As the story goes, the T'ang emperor had just returned from the court. He was drinking wine, enjoying the blossoms, when all at once he fell asleep and dreamed he saw a dragon king crying, "Emperor! Save my life! Save my life!"[33]

The girl played the *p'i-p'a* tune "Sobbing in the Moonlight," and continued to sing her story:

The emperor's river of pity flowed in the palace;[34]
He sent out gold tablets instructing all his officials:
"Be quick and summon the dragon-killing officer;
You Generals Black and White must both be diligent."
The stout cord of the emperor's words soon snapped;
The butterfly[35] *soared aloft and killed the old dragon.*
Could the Dragon King want to go anywhere without his head?
In the bright moonlight he rattled the gate of the silver palace.
Next day, too weary to mount his dragon horse and go to court,
The sage ruler summoned a doctor to his palace.
Devils came and took the emperor away for five days;
In nine hells, gloomy and dark, he stood before the dead.[36]

---

[32] These lines are obscure. They perhaps refer to the extermination of family members and followers of Li Chien-ch'eng and Li Yüan-chi. The Dragon is probably T'ang T'ai-tsung.

[33] In chapter 10 of *Journey to the West* the Dragon King of the Ching River disobeys a decree from the Court of Heaven in order to win a wager. Consequently, he is sentenced by Heaven to be decapitated by Wei Cheng, an official in the court of T'ang T'ai-tsung. The Dragon King beseeches the emperor for help, a request that T'ai-tsung attempts to honor by engaging Wei Cheng in a game of chess at the appointed hour for execution. Wei Cheng dozes off for a moment, however, and kills the Dragon King in a dream.

[34] This song gives a brief, if opaque, summary of events in *Journey to the West* up to the point where *The Tower of Myriad Mirrors* takes off.

[35] I.e., Wei Cheng, who, as already noted, killed the dragon in a dream. Butterfly is a figure for dream by way of allusion to Chuang-tzu, who once dreamed he was a butterfly and couldn't decide upon waking whether he was then a butterfly dreaming it was Chuang-tzu.

[36] T'ang T'ai-tsung, exhausted by the harassment of the Dragon King's ghost, is taken disembodied to the Underworld. There he appears before the ten kings of the Underworld to answer charges that he reneged on his promise to help the Dragon King (*Journey*, chapter 11).

A dark official, cheating, gave him extra days and months.[37]
The jade phoenix sounded again, life glimmered faintly.
Back and forth twixt life and death, then the T'ang Emperor
Again as before gazed over his realm.
He sighed and said, "How sad, how very sad—
"A hundred years of life on earth are but ephemeral.
Dismal souls below the well[38]*—when will they be saved?"*
Thus, the emperor asked the monk Ch'en Hsüan-tsang
To call to wayward, sunken souls with golden bell and jade chimes,
And chant with inky sleeves and banner black for souls to be reborn.
The Bodhisattva[39] *herself appeared to speak the Law*
And find a priest who'd seek the Western Sage.
The priest rode to the border of China;
In the Tiger House[40] *he grieved that Heaven so molds men.*
He climbed the Mountain of Two Frontiers, removed the Buddha seal,
And took a disciple[41] *at the foot of Five Phases Mountain.*
At Stone Brook the yellow dragon swallowed his purple deer;[42]
In fragrant wood white walls became red will-o'-the wisps.[43]
Wind blew into fiery eyes, the road to the West was obscured;
But Ling Chi came aflying, and a hundred troubles vanished.[44]
The wise monkey cast line five of the hexagram Opposition;[45]

---

[37] Ts'ui Chüeh, the Keeper of the Ledger of Life and Death in the Underworld, furtively adds two strokes to the characters for thirteen, the number of years of rule allotted to T'ai-tsung in the Ledger, thereby changing it to thirty-three. Thus T'ai-tsung, who properly should have died at that time, is given an extra twenty years of life.

[38] I.e., in the Underworld.

[39] I.e., Kuan-yin. This and the preceding three lines refer to the great mass for lost souls in the Underworld commissioned by T'ang T'ai-tsung (*Journey*, chapter 12). Hsüan-tsang is chosen to officiate because he is held by all to be a pure and learned monk.

[40] This refers to the home of Liu Po-ch'in, whom we met in chapter 4 (see note 3).

[41] Monkey.

[42] At Eagle's Grief Stream (*Journey*, chapter 15) a dragon swallows the white horse that the T'ang Priest had ridden from China. Kuan-yin changes the dragon into another white horse, the Priest's mount for the duration of the trip.

[43] The covetous abbot of Kuan-yin Temple attempts to acquire the T'ang Priest's gorgeous cassock, a gift of T'ang T'ai-tsung, by burning the Priest to death in a meditation hall of the temple (*Journey*, chapter 16). Monkey shields the Priest from harm and turns the tables by blowing the flames onto the rest of the temple.

[44] Battling to rescue his master from the Yellow Wind Demon (*Journey*, chapter 21), Monkey is stunned when the monster blasts him with a wind that forces his eyes shut (Monkey's eyes are fire-red from his forty-nine days in Lao-tzu's alchemical cauldron). Bodhisattva Ling-chi comes at Monkey's request to subdue the monster.

[45] This line doesn't refer to a specific event in *Journey to the West*. The hexagram *k'uei* (Opposition) in the *I Ching* expresses the principle that it is things of opposite nature,

Defeated along the way, Pigsy bowed to the old priest.
Sunset at the River of Flowing Sand, hissing was heard a thousand miles;
He of mixed consciousness joined the return to pure awareness.[46]
The globefish was, after all, a thing in the pond;
Slowly morning bells gave way to the dulcimer of desire.[47]
When the ginseng tree was uprooted, the mournful monkey screamed;[48]
The White-boned Lady[49] *stood in a lush forest.*
When Monkey left, the priest was changed to tiger;[50]
Then Bull became the second one to mourn.
A long night hung over Lotus-flower Jade Cave;[51]
Before White Deer Mountain he saluted the Star of Longevity.[52]

---

such as Heaven and Earth, male and female, that bring about unity and completion. The fifth line speaks of a companion who "bites through the skin," someone able to penetrate deeply and help bring about success. Since the second line of the couplet refers to Pigsy, and Pigsy and Monkey are of opposite natures—wood and metal, respectively—the reference to the Opposition hexagram may allude to Pigsy's joining the pilgrimage.

[46] Sandy, whose haunt has been the River of Flowing Sands, is spoken of as having mixed consciousness. Hence he is given the name of Wu-ching (Aware-of-Purity).

[47] In chapter 23 of *Journey*, Pigsy is enticed away from his monk's vows (morning bells are rung at a Buddhist temple) by a monster posing as a wealthy widow with three comely daughters to marry off. The globefish, capable of distending itself into a spherical form, is used here for Pigsy, he of enormous belly. "Things in the pond" is a figure of speech for the average person, unenlightened and subject to sensual appetites.

[48] At Long Life Mountain the pilgrims come to a Taoist temple housing a marvelous ginseng tree that puts forth fruit only once in nine thousand years (*Journey*, chapter 24–25). Monkey uproots the tree after being correctly accused of stealing the fruit, but later repents and asks Kuan-yin to restore the tree to life.

[49] This is a monster who deceives all but Monkey by transforming itself into a beautiful woman (*Journey*, chapter 27). Monkey kills it after being tricked twice, but is sent away by the T'ang Priest who, failing to recognize that it had been a monster, believes Monkey has taken innocent life.

[50] With Monkey dismissed, the T'ang Priest stumbles into the lair of the Yellow-Robed Monster (*Journey*, chapter 29), but is released by the monster's wife, an abducted princess of Precious Ivory Kingdom. The Priest carries a letter to the princess's father, who hadn't seen his daughter for thirteen years. Meanwhile, the monster decides to pay a visit to his father-in-law. In the guise of a handsome man, he accuses the Priest of being a monster and proves his point by changing him into a tiger.

[51] At Flat-Top Mountain (*Journey*, chapters 32–35) the T'ang Priest is captured by the two monsters of Lotus-flower Cave, King Gold Horn and King Silver Horn. It is to the two of them collectively that the bull who mourns probably refers, for they are finally routed by Monkey.

[52] Monkey enlists the help of the Star of Longevity in chapter 26 of *Journey* to persuade the T'ang Priest not to recite the charm that tightens the band Monkey wears on his head. White Deer Mountain, however, is not a place mentioned in this part of *Journey*, and the meaning of this line is unclear.

The T'ang Priest whirled and danced in the mad wind;[53]
The 'Brother of the Emperor' sank in the Black Water.[54]
Taoism and Buddhism needn't always be at odds;
Poisoned blood, black and yellow all alike, is empty.[55]
Metal couldn't conquer metal, heart and spirit were blocked;[56]
Water met water, the old monk was exhausted.[57]
Two hearts darkened heaven and earth;
A pair of Sage Monkeys deceived Kuan-yin.[58]
A banana leaf put out the fire on the mountain slope;[59]
Horse loosed from willow green, slowly on they went.
Delayed days and nights at the Tower of Myriad Mirrors,
Who knows when they'll see the Most Reverend of Heaven?

Ko-ch'iang-hua's song had ended. She leaned over her *p'i-p'a* and breathed a long sigh that floated off into the distance.

When Monkey in the fold of the hill heard the Tower of Myriad Mirrors mentioned, suspicion arose in his mind. He thought, "The

---

[53] The Red Boy spirits the T'ang Priest away in a tornado in chapter 40 of *Journey*.

[54] The Spirit of the River of Black Water poses as a ferryman to trap the T'ang Priest and drag him under the water to his abode (*Journey*, chapter 43).

[55] This couplet refers to the story of Cart-slow Kingdom (*Journey*, chapters 44–46), where three animal spirits posing as Taoists had won the ear of the king and subjected the land's Buddhist monks to servitude. Monkey defeats the spirits in a magic contest and lectures the court on the unity of the Three Religions, Confucianism, Taoism, and Buddhism. Poisoned blood probably refers to humankind, sullied by sensual cravings. Black is the color of Heaven and yellow the color of Earth. In Chinese thought Heaven, Man, and Earth form a triad symbolizing the forces of the cosmos. Here the author seems to be saying that Buddhists and Taoists alike view phenomenal existence as empty of any reality that can be said to transcend mere appearances.

[56] At Chin (metal)-tou Mountain (*Journey*, chapters 50–52) Monkey fights the Rhinoceros Monster in an effort to release his Master. Even the aid of an army of celestial warriors and a magical weapon from the Buddha come to naught against the Rhinoceros. He turns out to be Lao-tzu's ox, who has stolen Lao-tzu's Vajra (a Sanskrit word that means "the essence of metal") Chisel and come to earth in the form of a rhinoceros. It takes Lao-tzu to defeat the monster; and thus Monkey, associated with metal in five phases theory, is unable to conquer the metal of the monster.

[57] There is a stream in the Land of Women (*Journey*, chapter 53) whose water is drunk when the women, in the absence of men, wish to have children. The T'ang Priest, named River Float as an infant because he had been found tied to a plank adrift on a river, drinks of the stream and becomes pregnant. Hence, when water—the priest—met the stream's water, the ordeal was exhausting until Monkey stole some abortion water from a Taoist temple.

[58] This refers to Monkey's battle with the Six-eared Monkey.

[59] This is the episode of the Flaming Mountain recounted in the introduction (pp. 7–8).

Tower of Myriad Mirrors business happened to me just yesterday. How could she possibly know?" His temper flared. His anger grew. All he wanted was to strike Little Moon King dead so he could find out what was going on. And if you don't know what finally happened, heed the explanation in the next chapter.

CHAPTER THIRTEEN

Monkey Meets an Old Man in Green Bamboo Cave;
By the Reed Flowers Monkey Seeks the Emperor of Ch'in.

When Monkey heard the words "Tower of Myriad Mirrors" from the fold in the hill, a flame arose in his heart. He pulled his cudgel from behind his ear and jumped onto the tower, swinging wildly, but struck only air. He cursed Little Moon King and said, "What country's king are you that you dare to trap my Master here?"

Little Moon King looked as if he hadn't heard and went on smiling and chatting. Monkey cursed again, "You stinking blind women! What are you doing singing here with this hairy monk?"

It seemed as if the three singing girls hadn't heard either, so he shouted, "Master, let's get out of here!" But like the others, the T'ang Priest did not hear.

Monkey was astounded. He said, "Am I dreaming? Or is everyone in the Emerald Green World eyeless, earless, and tongueless? Ridiculous! Ridiculous! I'll try again to see if this is really the Master or not."

He assumed the form he had used to raise havoc in Heaven.[1] This time, however, it wouldn't do to be so brash, so he jumped to the opposite hill and took another good look. He saw that the T'ang Priest looked hopelessly depressed. Little Moon King was saying, "Don't think only of sad things, Mr. Ch'en. I ask you, what about that business of digging through to Heaven? If you've decided not to continue your journey, I'll dismiss the Sky-walkers and send them home."

The T'ang Priest said, "I hadn't made up my mind yesterday, but today I've decided not to go on."

Little Moon King was delighted. He at once sent someone to tell the Sky-walkers there was no more need to dig at the sky, and sent word for the singing girls to put on their make-up and give a performance. The

---

[1] When fighting the hosts of Heaven, Monkey transformed himself into a three-headed, six-armed apparition brandishing three cudgels.

singing girls knelt together and said, "Your Majesty, we cannot do an opera today."

Little Moon King said, "The calendar only says whether or not a day is favorable for sacrifices, for planting, for beginning school, for a capping ceremony, or for traveling. I've never seen an unfavorable day for giving a performance."

The girls replied, "It's not unfavorable, Your Majesty, it's impossible. Mr. Ch'en has ten thousand sorrows and a thousand knots of sadness. If we give a successful performance, he will be moved to tears."

Little Moon King cried, "What shall we do? Why don't you put on a modern play instead of an ancient play?"

The girls responded, "If you want an ancient play we'll do it, but we won't do a modern play."

Little Moon King snapped, "Rubbish! Today we're celebrating Mr. Ch'en's happy decision by having a great tea-banquet. How can we not have a performance? It would be lovely if you'd just do any plays you please."

The girls agreed and left. Two maids attending brought fresh tea from one side. The T'ang Priest sat down. From the back of the hall came a rolling of drums, a beating of gongs, a blast of horns, and much shouting. A clamor arose from the stage and the announcement came: "Today we'll perform a 'romantic' story called *Dream of Mist and Rain on Kao-t'ang Terrace*.[2] First we'll do the five scenes about Prime Minister Sun. It'll be terrific! Just terrific!"

Monkey, still hiding in the fold of the hill, heard this quite clearly. He thought, "There's a *Prime Minister Sun* and a *Dream on Kao-t'ang Terrace*. I suppose they won't leave till all the scenes have been played one by one. I might as well go find something to drink, then I'll come back and see my old monk."

Suddenly he heard footsteps behind him. He turned and saw a Taoist acolyte of about thirteen hissing at him, "Little Priest! Little Priest! I've come to watch the play with you."

Monkey laughed and said, "Hey little fellow, so you knew I was here and came to find me."

The acolyte said, "Don't tease me. My master is no one for you to make fun of."

Monkey said, "And what's your master called?"

The Taoist lad said, "He is the Master of Green Grove Cave, who loves guests and sightseeing jaunts."

---

[2] This refers to the erotic dream of King Hsiang of Ch'u. See note 7 in chapter 2.

Monkey laughed and said, "Wonderful! I must go and get some tea from him. You can sit here in my place for a while and watch the play and see if the party breaks up. I'll go to your honorable master's place and get something to quench my thirst. If they do break up, would you mind coming at once to tell me?"

The acolyte chuckled and said, "That's no trouble. There's nothing blocking the way into the cave—just let yourself in. I'll wait for you here."

Monkey was delighted. He entered the pitch-black cave and skipped along till he came to a bright stone grotto. There he ran smack into an old man, who asked, "Where do you come from, Priest? Please come in for some tea."

Monkey said, "If there were no tea, I wouldn't have come."

The old man smiled and said, "There's not necessarily tea, Priest. Why don't you go?"

Monkey said, "If there's no tea, I won't leave."

The two were like old friends. They walked, laughing as they went, till they had passed a stone stairway. There they came all at once to a fairy cave at the edge of a stream. Monkey said, "Have we reached your residence?

The old man said, "Not yet. This place is called 'Imitation of an Ancient Evening Landscape.'"

Monkey gazed at the scene. It was indeed a pleasant spot. On the left there stretched a field where random stones and about ten loquat trees with riotous branches and leaves surrounded a straw cottage. At its front door stood a great red pine and several maples entwined with mist. Their trunks and branches were woven into a stormy mountain forest. A bit of bamboo fence could be seen peeking through the trees, and two or three kinds of wildflowers poked out from the bottom of the fence.

A middle-aged man strolled by the stream, leaning on a moss-covered staff. Abruptly he sat down, and cupping the clear water in his hands, took it into his mouth and swished it around and around. He did this for a long while and then stood up. He looked toward the southwest and laughed casually.

When Monkey saw him laugh, he looked to the southwest himself. But he saw neither high tower nor green pavilion, dangerous cliffs or weird peaks. He saw only two splashes of mountain-color that looked like something between clouds and mist, between being and non-being.

All Monkey wanted was to have a drink of tea. How could he have any feeling for mountains and water? He and the old man walked right on and came upon another fairy cave. The old man said, "This isn't my cottage either. It's called 'Imitation of the Ancient T'ai-k'un Pond.'"

They were surrounded on all four sides by green peaks. Some of them lifted their faces as if looking at Heaven; some bent forward as if drinking the water; some seemed to be running, some sleeping; some looked as if they were whistling; some were sitting face-to-face like Confucian scholars; some looked like they were flying; some looked possessed by spirits; and some were like cows, horses, and sheep.

Monkey laughed and said, "All these stone people and stone horses are already carved, but no one has put up any tombstones. I guess there was no one to write the inscriptions."

The old man said, "Don't try to be funny, Little Priest. Take a look in the water."

Monkey bent his head to look carefully at the water and saw therein a hundred encircling green peaks. On the water's rippling surface they were as beautiful as a painting of mountains and forests.

While Monkey was engrossed in looking, several fishing boats darted out from behind one or two reeds. The people sitting in the bows of those boats were mostly old men with scraggly hair and dirty faces. It was hard to tell what they were singing—it wasn't the "Fisherman's Song" or the "Song of Picking Lotus." They sang:

Right nor wrong ever came to fishing spots;
Glory and shame follow men on horseback.
You, honored guest, seek the World of Oblivion?
Push the oars forward,
Pull slightly back
Look to the south, flutter the oars,
Push, push, then pull!

When Monkey heard the words "World of Oblivion," he asked the old man, "Where is this World of Oblivion?"

The old man said, "Who might you be looking for?"

Monkey said, "My relative, the First Emperor of Ch'in, recently moved to the World of Oblivion. I'd like to see him and have a word with him."

The old man said, "Well, if you want to go, just cross here. You'll come to a belt of green mountains. They are his back door."

Monkey said, "But if I go off in a world as big as this one, I won't be able to find him. I won't go."

The old man said, "The First Emperor of Ch'in is also an old friend of mine. If you're afraid to go, leave a message with me, and I'll give it to him when I see him tomorrow."

Monkey said, "I have another relative, the T'ang emperor, who wants to borrow a Mountain-removing Bell from my relative the First Emperor of Ch'in."

The old man said, "Oh, what rotten luck! Someone just borrowed it yesterday."

Monkey said, "Who borrowed it?"

The old man said, "It was loaned to Han Kao-tsu."[3]

Monkey laughed and said, "So, an old man like you lies like a youngster, eh? Han Kao-tsu was the First Emperor of Ch'in's mortal enemy. How could he borrow the bell?"

The old man said, "Don't you know, Little Priest, that by now the old enmity between Ch'in and Han has disappeared?"

Monkey said, "If that's so, when you see the First Emperor, tell him for me that in two days when Han Kao-tsu finishes using the bell I'll come to borrow it."

The old man said, "That'll be fine."

After chatting for a while, Monkey became even more thirsty. He cried out, "I want tea! Give me some tea!"

The old man smiled and said, "Since you're a relative of the First Emperor of Ch'in, and I'm an old friend of his, we are, after all, flesh and blood. If you want tea, I'll give you tea. If you want food, I'll give you food. Please come to my cottage."

The two of them passed beyond the green encircling peaks and, taking another path, arrived at the Fairy Cave of Green Bamboo. Green moss covered the ground; bamboo stalks stretched to the sky. In their midst stood four cottages of purple bamboo, and the two entered one of them straightaway. The main room's cross-beam was made of Hsiang River Goddess bamboo and its pillars of mud-green bamboo. The doors of the gate were of wind-man bamboo, flattened and stitched together. There was a square bamboo bed whose curtain was bamboo paper.

The old man went to the back of the room and brought out two bowls of magnolia-flower tea. Monkey took one in his hand, drank a few sips, and quenched his thirst. The old man prepared an oil-bamboo table

---

[3] I.e., Liu Pang, founder of the Han dynasty.

and four green bamboo chairs, and they sat down facing each other. The old man asked about Monkey's eight characters.[4]

Monkey laughed and said, "You and I met by chance. We are not sworn brothers and we don't want to match a marriage. Why do you want to know my eight characters?"

The old man said, "I tell fortunes by horoscope and I've never been wrong. Since you're a relative of my good friend the First Emperor of Ch'in, I want to tell your fortune and see what good luck you'll have in the future. This will be a favor to my friend."

Monkey lifted his head and thought. He said, "My eight characters are extremely good."

The old man said, "I haven't even worked it out yet. How can you already know they're good?"

Monkey said, "I've often asked people to tell my fortune. The year before last a black-robed fortune teller was going to tell my fortune, and when he heard my eight characters, he was startled. He stood up and bowed to me with his hands clasped, saying over and over, 'I beg your pardon! I beg your pardon!'

"Then he called me 'little official,' and said, 'These eight characters of yours are exactly those of the Great Sage, Equal of Heaven.' I remember that the Great Sage, Equal of Heaven went on a rampage in the Heavenly Palace and displayed his awesome spirit. Now he is soon to become a buddha. Since my eight characters are the same as his, how can they be bad?"

The old man said, "The Great Sage, Equal of Heaven was born on the first day of the first month in the first year of a sixty-year cycle."

Monkey said, "That's me. I was born on the first day of the first month in the first year of a sixty-year cycle."

The old man laughed and said, "They say if your appearance is good, your fate is good; if your fate is good, your appearance is good—this is indeed no mistake. There's no need to tell me your eight characters. Even your face is a monkey's."

Monkey said, "This Great Sage, Equal of Heaven—could it be that he has a monkey face too?"

The old man laughed and said, "You're not the real Great Sage, Equal of Heaven—you have *only* a monkey face. If you were really the Great Sage, Equal of Heaven, you'd be a monkey spirit!"

---

[4] A person's "eight characters" are the four pairs of characters denoting the year, month, day, and hour of his or her birth. The interrelationships between the characters are interpreted in the manner of a horoscope.

Monkey lowered his head and chuckled. He said, "Be quick, old man, and tell my fortune."

In fact, since Monkey was born from a stone egg he had never found out his own eight characters. His birth date was kept in a jade box in the Upper Palace, and was passed on only in the deep mountains and secret valleys. Now he was using this trick to bring it out. The old man wasn't wise to Monkey's scheme and began to relate his fortune.

"Little Priest," he said, "don't blame me if I don't flatter you to your face."

Monkey laughed and said, "It's better not to flatter me."

The old man said, "Your life was established in the key of D, enmity for you lies in G. Favor is found in the key of C, you dwell in the key of E, and difficulty comes in the key of A.[5] This month is re, and it clashes with the Star of Difficulty. Therefore, certain things will go wrong to make you angry. The Star of Augmented Fa also enters into your fate. Augmented Fa is the Goddess of the Moon. A scripture says, 'When one comes upon Augmented Fa, there will be a bizarre encounter. A beautiful girl will meet a handsome young man.'

"As for you, Little Priest, since you're a monk we shouldn't talk about matters of husband and wife—but in terms of your fate, you ought to get married."

Monkey responded, "How about that dry marriage I was involved in?"[6]

The old man said, "Marriage is marriage, dry or wet. It's all in your horoscope. Now, you will encounter the Star of La in the key of E. This is a beneficial star. Suddenly the Water Star of the Southern Palace becomes involved. This is another star of difficulty. A scripture says, 'When one meets both favor and difficulty at once, it's called "The Sea of Evil." A stone man or iron horse will find it difficult to bear.' Judging from this, you should have both the blessing of acquiring new family members and the sorrow of a relative's departure."

Monkey asked, "I added one master and left one master. Does that count?"

The old man said, "For a monk that will do. However, when this day is past, there will be more strange occurrences. Tomorrow you enter the Stars of Sol and La. You must kill people."

---

[5] Tung Yüeh is very original in using the names of traditional Chinese musical modes and pitches in this episode about fortune-telling. We are not aware that he made worked from any particular texts on fortune-telling or horoscopes.

[6] Since Monkey, as Beautiful Lady Yü, successfully resisted Hsiang Yü's amorous advances, their marriage was a "dry" one.

Monkey thought, "Killing people is a small matter . . . nothing to worry about."

The old man again said, "Three days from now you'll come into the Star of Augmented *Do*. A scripture says, 'Augmented *Do* is otherwise called the Star of Brightness. It will make even a weary, muddled old man clear and intelligent.' This is a case of benevolence in hardship and hardship in benevolence. The four great stars of change—Sun, Moon, Water, and Earth—will also enter your fate. I'm afraid, Little Priest, you must die once in order to live again."

Monkey laughed and said, "Life and death are nothing serious. If I must die, I'll be dead for a few years. If I must live, then I'll live for a year or two."

The two of them were thus entranced in conversation when the acolyte rushed in and shouted, "Little Priest! The play is almost finished. The Kao-t'ang dream is already over. Hurry! Hurry!"

Monkey quickly took leave of the old man, thanked the acolyte, and returned the same way he had come. When he got to the fold in the hill, he peered into the tower and heard, "There's still one part of *Dream on Kao-t'ang Terrace* to go." He strained his eyes to watch the play.

On the stage he saw a Taoist and five immortals. The Taoist said, "A Taoist who wished to save the ignorant fully explained men's desires and the ways of the world. Keep this in your hearts when you wake from your dreams, you people of the world."

Then Monkey heard the people on stage rumble, "*The Dream of South Branch*[7] is tedious. Only *Prime Minister Sun* is ever played well. Prime Minister Sun is no other than Sun Wu-k'ung. Look! His wife is so beautiful, his five sons so dashing. He started out as a monk, but came to such a good end! Such a very good end!"

---

[7] This refers to the story of a man who in the space of a few seconds dreams that he passes an entire lifetime.

CHAPTER FOURTEEN

Young Lord T'ang Accepts an Order to Lead the Troops;
Lady Green-twine Becomes a Broken Jade by the Pool.

Monkey heard all this clearly from the fold of the hill. He said, "I've been single and chaste since I was born from the stone egg. When was I married to any woman? When did I ever have five children? It must be that Little Moon King really likes my Master and can't get him to stay here. Since he was afraid the Master was thinking about me, what he did was to slander me and write this play saying I'd become a high official, husband, and father. He's trying to get the Master to change his mind and forget about the West. But I mustn't be too hasty—I'll watch and see what happens."

At that moment he heard the T'ang Priest say, "I don't want to see any more plays. Ask Lady Green-twine to come here."

A maid immediately brought in a jade flying-cloud teapot and a teacup painted with scenes from the Hsiao and Hsiang Rivers. Shortly, Lady Green-twine entered. She was indeed an exotic beauty who could not be matched in a thousand years, whose fragrance wafted for ten miles.

In his fold of the hill Monkey thought, "When people on earth speak of beauty, they speak in comparison to Bodhisattva Kuan-yin. Now, I haven't seen the Bodhisattva often—maybe ten or twenty times—but seeing this lady, it almost seems the Bodhisattva could be her disciple. I wonder what the Master will do when he sees her."

Lady Green-twine had just been seated when Pigsy and Sandy appeared behind her. The T'ang Priest said angrily, "Chu Wu-neng! Last night you peeped from the Little Animal Palace and startled my beloved lady. I've dismissed you. What are you doing here?"

Pigsy said, "The ancients said, 'Great anger doesn't last the night.' Young Lord Ch'en, please forgive me this time."

The T'ang Priest said, "Well, if you don't go, I'll write a bill of separation to send you away."

Sandy said, "Young Lord Ch'en, if you want to drive us off, we'll leave. When a husband wants to get rid of his wife, he has to write a bill of divorce. But when a master wants to dismiss disciples there's no need for that."

Pigsy said, "There's no harm in it—these days there are many masters and disciples who are husband and wife. But where does Young Lord Ch'en expect us two to go?"

The T'ang Priest said, "You return to your wife. Sandy can go back to the River of Flowing Sand."

Sandy said, "I'm not going to the River of Flowing Sand. I'll go to the Mountain of Flowers and Fruit to be a Counterfeit Monkey."

The T'ang Priest said, "Wu-k'ung has been made a prime minister. Where is he now?"

Sandy said, "He's not a prime minister any more. He's following another master and continuing toward the West."

The T'ang Priest said, "If that's so, you two will surely run into him on the road. By all means stop him from coming to bother me here." He asked for a brush and ink-stone and began to write the bill of separation:

Wu-neng is my thief; were I to keep a thief, I'd be sheltering a thief. If I don't shelter the thief, he won't have a home. If the thief doesn't cling to me, I'll be clean. If the thief and I remain together, we'll both become thieves. If the thief and I separate, we'd both benefit. I don't love you, Wu-neng—leave quickly.

Pigsy took the bill of separation mournfully. The T'ang Priest again wrote:

The writer of this bill of separation is Ch'en Hsüan-tsang, beloved brother of Little Moon King. The appearance of the Monster-monk Sandy is very grim. He has not cast off his mixed consciousness so he is not my disciple. Today I dismiss him. I won't see him again till we go to the Yellow Spring. Witnessed by Little Moon King and Lady Green-twine.

Sandy, too, was very sad as be accepted his bill of separation. The two of them went out of the tower together and left. The T'ang Priest was unconcerned. He laughed and said to Little Moon King, "I'm rather a nuisance, am I not?" Then he asked, "Lady Green-twine, what has happened since this morning?"

Lady Green-twine replied, "I was feeling depressed so I wrote a song to the tune of 'Crow's Nest.' I'd like to sing it for you." She gathered up her sleeves and knitted her eyebrows. In a lilting voice she sang:

Three, five stars in the bright moon of the sixteenth;
"Ding, ding," chimes the water clock, "thrum, thrum," sounds the drum.
No bridge o'er the Milky Way[1] for our mutual love;
This pitiful girl passes a pitiful night.

Her song ended, she was overcome by sorrow. "My Young Lord," she cried, "our relationship is finished." She embraced the T'ang Priest miserably. The T'ang Priest was alarmed and tried to comfort her with pleasant words.

Lady Green-twine sobbed and said, "How can you be like this when separation is at hand?" She pointed with one finger and said, "Look to the south, Young Lord, and you'll know what I mean."

The T'ang Priest turned his head to see a band of mounted soldiers galloping toward them carrying a yellow banner. He began to feel uneasy. Before long the tower was filled with soldiers on horseback. One officer in a purple robe carried an imperial decree. He saluted the T'ang Priest and said, "I am a messenger from New T'ang." He ordered, "Soldiers, help the Supreme Commander into uniform."[2]

They quickly set up an incense table. The T'ang Priest knelt facing northward, and the purple-robed officer, facing south, read the decree. After he finished reading, the officer took out a five-colored tally and gave it to the T'ang Priest, saying, "There can be no delay, General. The enemy from the West is at hand. Bring out your troops immediately."

The T'ang Priest said, "You have no tact, officer. You may wait until I've taken leave of my family." He turned and went to the back of the hall to look for Lady Green-twine. She had watched him being made a general, and now, prepared to depart on his journey, he seemed pressed for time. Embracing him with both arms she wept and collapsed to the floor. She said, "How can I let you go, Young Lord? Your body is sick and feeble. A general spends his days on windy mountains and sleeps in damp valleys. There will be no relative to look after you and tell you when to put on an extra unlined robe or take off one of your white sashes. You'll have to take care of yourself and adjust for the cold. Young

---

[1] The "bridge o'er the Milky Way" again alludes to the story of the Spinning Lady and the Cowherd. See note 9 in chapter 2.

[2] A general would normally be in formal uniform to receive an imperial order.

Lord, always remember what I say at our parting: don't use harsh punishment on your soldiers and officers for fear they might do you evil; be careful in accepting surrendered soldiers for fear they might rob your camp; don't rush heedlessly into dark forests. If the horses whinny at sunset, don't keep going. If in spring there are flowers on the riverbank, don't step on them. If there are cool nights in summer, don't stay out in the breeze. When you're depressed, don't think about today; but when you're happy, don't forget me.

"Alas, my Lord, how can I let you go? Were I to go with you, I fear it would violate your orders. But if I let you go alone, my Lord, don't you know how long the sad windy nights will be? It's better my fragile soul should join you in your jade general's tent."

The T'ang Priest and Lady Green-twine joined in a tight embrace and wailed. They swayed in each other's arms till they fell beside the Pool of Broken Jade.

Lady Green-twine threw herself into the water. The T'ang Priest wept bitterly and called, "Lady! Lady! Come back to me!"

The purple-robed officer galloped in and whisked the T'ang Priest away, and the whole army hurried toward the west.

CHAPTER FIFTEEN

The T'ang Priest Musters His Troops Under the Midnight Moon;
The Great Sage's Spirit Falters Before the Banners of Five Colors.

It was already evening when from the fold of the hill Monkey saw that his Master had indeed become a general. The matter of getting the scriptures had been shelved, and Monkey was left quite bewildered. He could think of nothing to do but take on the guise of a soldier and mingle with the troops. He passed a troubled night.

At dawn the next morning, the T'ang Priest sat in his tent and ordered soldiers to raise the banner saying, "Enlisting Soldiers. Buying Horses." A soldier carried out the order, and by noon the new recruits and officers numbered two million. Another troubled day passed for Monkey.

The T'ang Priest appointed a minor general of the White Banner, also called his 'minor personal general,' who that night gave orders to build a gold-chained commander's platform and to compile a register of soldiers' names. He then ordered a roll call to be made from the platform on the next evening.

The next night at the third watch the moon shone bright as day. The T'ang Priest ascended the platform and issued orders for all his generals, saying: "Tonight my roll call of officers and soldiers won't be the same as in the past. When one toll of the bell is heard, all soldiers will prepare their meals. When the bell is tolled twice, armor must be put on. When the bell tolls thrice, all should resolve their wills and rouse their spirits. At four tolls of the bell, the men should assemble beneath the platform for muster."

The minor general of the White Banner received the order and told the other officers, "Pay heed and spread the order, officers. Tonight's roll call will be unusual. When one toll of the bell is heard, all soldiers are to prepare their meals. When the bell is sounded twice, armor must be put on. When the bell sounds thrice, resolve your wills and rouse your spirits.

At four tolls of the bell, assemble beneath the platform for muster. There is to be no delay."

To which every officer and soldier in the whole camp responded, "If the commander gives an order, who dares disobey?"

The T'ang Priest again commanded, "White Banner, this is an order: The officers and men are not to call me 'Commander,' they are to call me 'Reverend Commander.'" The Minor General of the White Banner relayed the order throughout the camp.

The bell on the platform was sounded once. When the officers and soldiers heard it, they quickly prepared their food. The T'ang Priest again commanded, "Little General of the White Banner, relay this order to all my officers: When I give the roll call, bring all your training to bear. Don't be lackadaisical about falling in and don't wander aimlessly."

The bell on the platform rang twice, and the officers and soldiers hurriedly strapped on their armor. The T'ang Priest commanded, "White Banner, raise the banner for the roll call. Send the order to all regiments that waterways and mountain gorges are to be strictly controlled. Anyone allowing a freelance strategist who speaks or dresses irregularly into the camp will be beheaded." White Banner followed the command and relayed the order across the camp.

The T'ang Priest again commanded, "White Banner, give this order to the officers and the men: If anyone is not present at the roll call, he will lose his head. The same for anyone passing in front of the commander's gate. Anyone who pretends to be sick or looks to the left or right will lose his head. Anyone who recommends himself will lose his head. Anyone who goes ahead of his turn will lose his head. Anyone jumping or shouting will lose his head. So will anyone who hides something from his superiors, or takes someone else's place. Anyone whispering into another's ear will lose his head. Anyone who brings a girl or lets his thoughts wander or daydreams will lose his head. The same for anyone who lacks fierce determination, or loses his temper and starts a quarrel."

When these orders had been given, the bell on the platform rang out three times. Every man in the regiments focused his resolve and stirred his fighting spirit. The T'ang Priest, too, closed his eyes and sat quietly on the platform beneath the bright moon.

An hour later four rings of the bell sounded. From all camps the officers and men assembled before the platform for muster. One could see:

Banners and flags in perfect formation,
Swords and spears formed a forest.

Banners and flags in perfect formation,
Arrayed like the twenty-eight constellations—
Dipper banner on the left,
Cowherd on the right—
Every constellation distinct.
Swords and spears formed a forest,
Arranged like the sixty-four hexagrams—
Heaven's axes in odd-numbered lines,
Axes of earth in the even—
Every line in place.
At the first roar of the precious swords,
Fierce tigers on ten thousand mountains fell silent.
Scales on armor of rhinoceros-hide
Made the Five Seas' gold dragons seem pale.
Each one of them a malevolent star;
Every voice, the crashing of thunder.

The T'ang Priest followed the roll-book and called each name in order. He shouted, "You officers and men, now that I'm in the army, I can have no compassion. Every one of you must pay attention to avoid the axe." He immediately waved a flag to signal the order, and shouted the names of six thousand, six hundred and five of his troops in a row.

Then he came to "Great General Chu Wu-neng." The moment the T'ang Priest saw the name, he knew it was Pigsy. But in the army one must be quite serious; it doesn't do to show you know someone. He shouted, "You, General—so ugly and fierce. You must be a monster trying to deceive me. White Banner, push that fellow out and cut off his head."

Pigsy kowtowed again and again while saying, "Reverend Commander, cool your anger! Allow me one word before I die." And he said:

My surname is Chu (Pig),
Born eighth in my clan.
I followed the T'ang Priest to the Western Land,
But midway he wrote a bitter bill of separation.
I went to seek refuge in my father-in-law's village,
But I found that my wife had returned to Dry Ditch,
Returned to Dry Ditch.
So I turned once more and walked toward the West
And blundered into the Commander's camp.
I kneel in hope that the Commander will spare me
To work as a scullery in his camp.

A tiny smile crossed the T'ang Priest's face, and he ordered White Banner to release the bonds. Pigsy kowtowed a hundred times, thanking the T'ang Priest.

The name "Woman General Hua K'uei" was called. A woman officer carrying a sword galloped out of formation. Indeed she was:

A beautiful girl of sixteen, body smooth as cheese,
She'll breathe the essence of Heaven and Earth till both go dry.
A flying dragon sword hangs from her waist,
Only for killing those handsome, lustful men.

The name "Great General Sun Wu-k'ung" was called. The T'ang Priest blanched and gazed below his platform. It happened that Monkey had mixed amongst the army for the past three days in the form of a six-eared monkey soldier. When he heard the three words "Sun Wu-k'ung" he leaped out of formation and knelt on the ground, saying, "Little General Sun Wu-k'ung is transporting supplies and couldn't be present. I'm his brother Sun Wu-huan, and I wish to take his place in battle. In this I dare disobey the Commander's order."

The T'ang Priest said, "Sun Wu-huan, what is your origin? Tell me quickly, and I'll spare your life."

Hopping and dancing, Monkey said:

In the old days I was a monster,
Who took the name of Monkey.
After the Great Sage left the T'ang Priest,
I became his close relation by way of marriage.
There's no need to ask my name,
I'm the Six-eared Monkey, Great General Sun Wu-huan.

The T'ang Priest said, "The six-eared ape used to be Monkey's enemy. Now he's forgotten the old grudge and become generous. He must be a good man." He ordered White Banner to give Sun Wu-huan a suit of the iron armor of the vanguard and appointed him "Vanguard General to Destroy Entrenchment."

When the roll of officers and soldiers was concluded, the T'ang Priest quickly handed down an order. The troops were to form the beautiful-lady-seeking-her-husband formation to take advantage of the bright moon for their attack on the Western Barbarians. Once the troops had crossed the border into the land of the Western Barbarians, the T'ang Priest ordered officers and soldiers alike to display a small yellow banner as an identifying mark so they wouldn't become confused. The banners were fixed in place and the march continued.

Just as they came around a mountain, they confronted a band of horsemen carrying green banners. Since Monkey was general of the vanguard, he immediately jumped to the front of the ranks. From the midst of the green banner horsemen emerged a general in a purple helmet, carrying a sword to meet his enemy.

Monkey demanded, "Who comes?"

The general said, "I'm King Pāramitā.[1] Who are you that dares to challenge me?"

Monkey said, "I'm Sun Wu-huan, in the vanguard of he who carries the seal 'Great T'ang's Supreme Commander for Wiping out Desire.'"

King Pāramitā said, "I am the great honey king[2] who would dethrone your great sugar king." He whipped out his sword and struck.

Monkey said, "So—such a pitiful, nameless little general as you wants to soil my cudgel? He raised his cudgel to meet the blow.

They fought several rounds. No one could tell who was winning when King Pāramitā said, "Hold it! If I don't tell you about my family, when I kill you and you become a ghost, you'll still think I'm just a nameless little general. Allow me to explain: I, King Pāramitā, am none other than a direct descendant of Monkey Sun, the Great Sage, Equal of Heaven, who caused a great uproar in Heaven."

Monkey heard this and thought, "Strange ... Is it possible that the play given the other day was real? Here is the evidence before my eyes. How can it be false? But I don't know where my other four sons are and if my wife is still alive. If she's not dead, I wonder what she's doing now. And I don't know if this is my youngest son or the eldest. I'd like to ask him for details, but the Master's orders are very strict and I dare not disobey. I'll sound him out a bit more."

So he shouted, "Monkey is my sworn brother, and he never told me he had any children. How can he suddenly have a son?"

King Pāramitā said, "I see you still don't understand. I, King Pāramitā, and my father, Monkey, are a father and son who have never met. My father, Monkey, was originally a monster who lived in the

---

[1] Pāramitā is Sanskrit for "perfection." In Mahayana Buddhism a bodhisattva attains six (or ten in some schools) pāramitās as he works to achieve Nirvana.

[2] In the Chinese transliteration for *pāramitā*, the character used to render the syllable "mi" has the intrinsic meaning of "honey," while the character *t'ang* in T'ang dynasty is homophonous with the character meaning "sugar." King Pāramitā is punning on these associations.

Water-curtain Cave. He had a sworn brother, my uncle, called Demon Bull King. My uncle doesn't sleep with his first wife, Lady Rakshas. That woman, who lives in Banana Cave, is my mother. When a T'ang Priest from the southeast wanted to go to the Western Paradise and meet the Buddha, he asked my father, Monkey, to be his disciple. They had encountered numberless hardships on the road to the West, when one day they came upon Flaming Mountain. The Master and his several disciples fretted and grieved to no end.

"Then my father had a good idea. He said, 'A Master for one day is a father for life. I'll temporarily forget my vows of loyalty to my sworn brother in order to repay my Master's kindness.' He went at once to the Banana Cave. First he changed himself into the Demon Bull King and deceived my mother. Later he changed into a tiny insect and entered my mother's belly. He stayed there a while and caused her no end of agony. When my mother could no longer bear the pain, she had no choice but to give the Banana-leaf Fan to my father, Monkey. When my father, Monkey, got the Banana-leaf Fan, he cooled the inferno at Flaming Mountain and left.[3] In the fifth month of the next year, my mother suddenly gave birth to me, King Pāramitā. Day by day I grew older and more intelligent. If you think about it, since my uncle and mother had never been together, and I was born after my father, Monkey, had been inside my mother's belly, the fact that I am his direct descendant is beyond dispute."

After this story Monkey was between tears and laughter. Just then, thoroughly confused, he saw to the northwest Little Moon King bringing a column of soldiers, distinguishable by their purple battle dress, to relieve the T'ang Priest. From the southwest came a column of devil soldiers under a black banner to assist King Pāramitā.

King Pāramitā's troops were fierce. They charged headlong into the T'ang Priest's lines and killed Little Moon King. Then turning, they cut off the head of the T'ang Priest.

Confusion reigned. There was much killing amongst the four armies, and Monkey didn't know what to do. He could only watch, spellbound. He saw the black banners fall in amongst the ranks of the purple banners. Purple banners lay across green banners. One green banner flew into the purple banners. Purple banners marched into the ranks of the yellow banners. Yellow banners angled into the black

---

[3] To this point, King Pāramitā is recounting the episode that takes place in chapters 59–61 of *Journey to the West*, the antecedent of the present narrative.

banners. A large black banner[4] fell from the sky onto the yellow banners, killing yellow bannermen. Yellow bannermen rushed into the ranks of the green banners and seized several green banners, which were snatched away in turn by purple bannermen. Purple bannermen killed their own men. Several hundred purple banners fell into the blood and were dyed lichee-red. These were gathered by yellow bannermen into their ranks. Green bannermen marched into the troops under black banners and killed a number of them. Several small black banners flew into the air and fell onto a pine tree, while a million men in the ranks of yellow banners fell into a pit. A hundred small yellow command banners flew in amongst the small green command banners, and they blended into the color of duck's-head green. Sixteen or seventeen small purple command banners fell in with the green banners, and the green banner troops threw them into the air. They fell onto the troops of the black banners and disappeared.

Now Monkey was enraged. He couldn't control himself.

---

[4] Large and small banners denote high and low ranks.

CHAPTER SIXTEEN

The Elder of the Void Rouses Monkey from His Dream;
When the Great Sage Returns, the Sun Is Half Hidden in the Mountains.

Unable to control himself, Monkey changed into the three-headed, six-armed form in which he had rebelled in the Heavenly Palace. He struck out wildly in the air.

From behind someone called loudly, "Is Wu-k'ung no longer aware of vacuity? Is Wu-huan no longer aware of illusion?"[1]

Monkey turned his head and asked, "What country's general are you, that you dare to address me?" Looking up he saw an elder sitting on a lotus platform.

The elder called again, "Sun Wu-k'ung, aren't you awake yet?"

Monkey stopped swinging his cudgel and asked, "Who are you?"

The elder replied, "I'm the Master of the Void. I've watched you living in this false universe for quite some time, and I've come specially to rouse you. At this moment your real Master is hungry."

Monkey began to wake up a bit. It seemed that what had happened was all an illusion. He concentrated his whole mind, shutting out what had gone before, and begged the Master for instruction.

The Master of the Void said, "You've been snared in the aura of the Ch'ing Fish."

Monkey asked, "What kind of demon is this Ch'ing Fish that he can create a universe?"

The Master of the Void said, "When Heaven and Earth first split apart, the pure essence ascended, and the turbid sank. The half-pure and half-turbid remained in the middle, and that is man. What was mostly pure and only in small measure turbid gravitated to the Mountain of Flowers and Fruit, giving birth to Wu-k'ung. That which was mostly

---

[1] The literal meanings of the names Wu-k'ung and Wu-huan are "aware of vacuity" and "aware of illusion," respectively.

turbid and only in small measure pure gravitated to Little Moon Cave, giving birth to the Ch'ing Fish. The Ch'ing Fish and Wu-k'ung were born in the same hour, the only difference was that Wu-k'ung belonged to goodness, while the Ch'ing Fish belonged to evil. But the Ch'ing Fish's supernatural powers are ten times greater than Wu-k'ung's, and his body is extremely large. When he takes K'un-lun Mountains as a pillow for his head, his feet rest in the Kingdom of Dark Oblivion. Now he finds the World of Reality too small for him, so he dwells in the World of Illusion, which he calls the Emerald Green World."

Monkey said, "What are illusion and reality?"

The Master said, "There are three parts to creation: one part is No-Illusion, one part is Illusion, and one is Reality." Then he chanted this hymn:

> No springtime lads and lasses played;
> They were the root of the Ch'ing Fish.
> No New Emperor ever lived;
> He was the energy of the Ch'ing Fish.
> No green bamboo broom ever swept the hall;
> That was the name of the Ch'ing Fish.
> No general's commission was ever issued;
> It was the pattern of the Ch'ing Fish.
> No sky-gouging axes ever struck through;
> They were the form of the Ch'ing Fish.
> No Little Moon King ever lived;
> He was the spirit of the Ch'ing Fish.
> No Tower of Myriad Mirrors stood tall;
> It was the creation of the Ch'ing Fish.
> No man in the mirror ever beckoned;
> That was the body of the Ch'ing Fish.
> No Headache World ever existed;
> It was the construction of the Ch'ing Fish.
> No Green Pearl's tower was ever erected;
> It was the heart of the Ch'ing Fish.
> No Hsiang Yü of Ch'u ever strode forth;
> He was the soul of the Ch'ing Fish.
> No Beautiful Lady Yü ever died;
> She was a delusion of the Ch'ing Fish.
> King Yama was never absent from Hell;
> His was the world of the Ch'ing Fish.
> The World of the Ancients never existed;
> It was a fabrication of the Ch'ing Fish.
> Nor did the World of the Future exist;

It was the congealing of the Ch'ing Fish.
No Limitation Hexagram Palace stood firm;
It was the place of the Ch'ing Fish.
No Young Lord of T'ang ever went to war;
He was the sport of the Ch'ing Fish.
Singing and dancing were never indulged in;
That was the nature of the Ch'ing Fish.
No Lady Green-twine ever wept;
She was the exhaustion of the Ch'ing Fish.
No roll call platform was ever built;
It was the movement of the Ch'ing Fish.
No battle with Pāramitā ever ensued;
That was the brawling of the Ch'ing Fish.
For there is no Ch'ing Fish;
There is simply Monkey's desire.

When he finished, a great gust of wind arose and blew Monkey back to the mountain path. And he saw that the sun above the peony tree had barely moved.

It happened that when the real T'ang Priest awoke from his spring nap he found the boys and girls had already gone away. He was quite pleased, except that he didn't see Monkey. He woke Pigsy and Sandy and asked where Monkey had gone. Sandy said, "I don't know." Pigsy said, "I don't know."

All at once they saw Mu-ch'a, an attendant of Bodhisattva Kuan-yin, and a fair-faced monk riding an auspicious cloud and coming from the southwest. It fluttered down, and Mu-ch'a said, "T'ang Priest, take this new disciple. The Great Sage will return in a little while."

The T'ang Priest jumped to his feet and kowtowed. Mu-ch'a said, "Bodhisattva Kuan-yin is concerned about your hardship on the Western Road and sends this little disciple to join you here. However he's very young so the Bodhisattva urges your reverence to watch after him. The Bodhisattva has already given him the religious name Wu-ch'ing (Aware-of-Desire). She says that although Wu-ch'ing is your reverence's fourth disciple, he should be placed second only to Wu-k'ung and above Wu-neng in order to complete the phrase, "make empty of desire and be purified."[2] The T'ang Priest accepted the Bodhisattva's order and took in the disciple, then saw Mu-ch'a off.

---

[2] This phrase is composed of the second characters in the religious names of Monkey (Wu-k'ung), the new disciple (Wu-ch'ing), Pigsy (Wu-neng), and Sandy (Wu-ching). This line *"k'ung ch'ing neng ching"* is especially enigmatic. We translate it to reflect the

The Ch'ing Fish demon had in fact distracted the Mind-Monkey with the sole intention of devouring the T'ang Priest.[3] Thus, while he entangled the Great Sage, he also changed his shape to that of a little monk to ensnare the Priest. How was he to know that the Great Sage had been awakened by the Elder of the Void? This shows that though evil demons use a thousand schemes, one whose mind is straight need fear no demon.

When Monkey returned through the air, he spied the little monk sitting by his Master. The monk's evil aura rose ten thousand feet, and Monkey knew right off that he was a transformation of the Ch'ing Fish. He took his cudgel from behind his ear and struck without a second thought. In an instant the little monk had turned into the corpse of a mackerel.[4]

A beam of red light issued from the corpse's mouth. Monkey followed it with his eyes, and he saw a tower appear within the red beam. In the tower stood the Hegemon of Ch'u. He shouted, "I beg your leave, Beautiful Lady Yü!" Then the beam of red light passed to the southeast and disappeared.

The T'ang Priest said, "Wu-k'ung, I'm famished!"

When Monkey heard this, he quickly turned and with his hands clasped made a great bow toward his Master. He repeated what had just happened from beginning to end.

Now when the T'ang Priest had found Monkey missing, he was at first quite anxious. But when Monkey returned and straight off killed his new disciple, he grew angry and was about to reprimand him. Then he saw that the new disciple had become a mackerel corpse. He quickly realized that Monkey's intentions were good, while the new disciple had been a demon. And when he heard Monkey describe the fierceness of the

---

Buddhist perspective, with *ch'ing* being read as "desire." To a proponent of the political interpretation, however, the sentence can mean nothing but, "Annihilate the Ch'ing dynasty and the land will be purified." Given Tung Yüeh's interest in medicine, still another level of meaning is possible. *K'ung ch'ing* is the name of a medicinal plant whose properties are said to be effective in the cure of blindness. It is green on the outside and hollow in the center, the latter quality an apt metaphor for the spiritual condition sought by the adherent of Ch'an. With this in mind, the original sentence suggests that one attains purity in the image of this empty plant which is by nature a remedy for blindness.

[3] In *Journey to the West* all manner of monsters and demons try to devour the Tang Priest, because to eat even a bit of his flesh would assure them immortality.

[4] Mackerel is the literal meaning of the Chinese term *ch'ing yü* (Ch'ing Fish). See also chapter 1 note 1.

demon, his anger changed to joy. He said, "You've been through a lot of trouble, Disciple."

Pigsy said, "Wu-k'ung just went to play. If that's trouble, then when we really meet trouble the Master will call it play."

The T'ang Priest made Pigsy be quiet and asked Monkey, "Wu-k'ung, you say you passed several days in the Emerald Green World. Why has it not even been an hour here?"

Monkey said, "Though the mind is deluded, time is not."

The T'ang Priest said, "I wonder which is longer—mind or time?"

Monkey said, "When mind is short, it is Buddha. When time is short, it is a demon."

Sandy said, "The demon has been destroyed. The world is pure and empty. Brother, why don't you go to the village again and beg for some food? Let the Master sit for a while with a quiet mind, then we'll start again on the Western road."

Monkey said, "All right," and walked on ahead. He had gone just a short way when he ran into the local mountain deity. Monkey cursed him, "How insolent you are! I was looking for you the other day to ask you something, but when I said the magic words you never came. What kind of great local deity are you anyway? Quick! Stick out your leg and I'll give it a hundred whacks. Then we'll sort it out."

The deity begged him. "Lord Great Sage, just then you were dragged beyond Heaven by the Demon of Desire. My powers are limited. How could I go beyond Heaven to kowtow to you? Please, Great Sage, weigh my merit against this guilt."

Monkey said, "What merit do you claim?"

The deity replied, "I took your flower ball from Lord Pigsy's ear."

Monkey dismissed him. Then, intent on begging for food, he leaped into the air. To one side he saw a path covered with peach blossoms. A wisp of smoke rose indistinctly from amidst the wood. Immediately he lowered his cloud to take a look. Finding it to be a nice house, Monkey went inside and was looking for someone he could ask for food when he came upon a quiet room. There sat a master who had gathered several disciples around him and was explicating a text. Can you guess which line he was explaining? He was discussing none other than: "It encompasses Heaven and Earth and nothing escapes it."[5]

---

[5] This is taken from an almost identical line in the "The Great Treatise" of the *I Ching*: "It encompasses all the transformations in the heavens and on earth, so that nothing escapes it." Here, "it" refers to the *I Ching*, which was believed to contain the principles underlying all phenomena. By partially quoting this line, Tung Yüeh seems to be saying that desire, too, encompasses all things.

Tung Yüeh's Answers to Questions on
THE TOWER OF MYRIAD MIRRORS

Q. *Journey to the West* is not incomplete; why a supplement?

A. *The Tower of Myriad Mirrors* comes after the episode "Flaming Mountain and the Banana-leaf Fan" (chapter 61) and before "Cleansing the Heart and Sweeping the Pagoda" (chapter 62). The Great Sage[1] devised a scheme to obtain the Banana-leaf Fan and cool the flames.[2] In this he merely uses his physical strength. The forty-eight-thousand years[3] are the amassed roots of desire. To become enlightened and open to the Great Way, one must first empty and destroy the roots of desire. To empty and destroy the roots of desire one must first go inside desire. After going inside desire and seeing its emptiness, one can then go outside it and realize the reality of the root of the Way. *The Tower of Myriad Mirrors* deals with the Demon of Desire, and the Demon of Desire is the Ch'ing Fish.

Q. The original text of *Journey to the West* has a million monsters. They all want to butcher the T'ang Priest and eat his flesh. In *The Tower of Myriad Mirrors,* the Ch'ing Fish merely enchants the Great Sage. Why is this?

A. Mencius said, "There is no better way of learning than to seek your own strayed heart."

Q. The original *Journey to the West* always begins an episode by telling what monster or evil spirit will be encountered. Your description of the Demon of Desire doesn't make clear at the beginning that it is in fact the Demon of Desire. Why is this?

---

[1] I.e., Monkey.

[2] *The Tower of Myriad Mirrors* was conceived as a supplement to be read in the context of events that transpire in chapters 59 to 61 of *Journey to the West.* There, master and disciples had found their route blocked by a flaming mountain, and Monkey had to battle the Demon Bull King and dupe Lady Rakshas to wrest from them a fan capable of suppressing the flames. See introduction, pp. 7-8.

[3] This perhaps refers to the time since the beginning of human history.

A. This is the main point of departure for *The Tower of Myriad Mirrors*.
For men, desire is a demon without form, without sound—a man
may not be conscious of it or know about it. It may enter by way of
grief, indulgence, a single doubtful or vacillating thought, or sensory
perceptions. It seems as if the desire that enters the sphere of your
thoughts cannot be stopped or changed or ignored; as if once it
enters it can in no way be expelled. But to recognize desire as a
demon is to achieve success. Therefore, when the Great Sage was in
the belly of the Ch'ing Fish, he didn't know it. Moreover, he didn't
know when he leapt out of the Ch'ing Fish that he would shortly
kill it. The deluded man and the enlightened one were not two
different people.

Q. In your novel the World of the Ancients is concerned with the past.
The World of the Future is concerned with the future. But how in
the days of early T'ang[4] can you have the soul of the Sung Prime
Minister Ch'in Kuei being punished?

A. *The Tower of Myriad Mirrors* is a dream of desire. If, for example, on
the third of the first month, you see in a dream that you will be in a
fight and receive wounds to your hands and feet on the third of the
third month and when the third of the third month arrives and you
are, in fact, in a fight, what your eyes see is no different from what
you dreamed. The third of the first month is not the third of the
third month. Rather, what you dreamed and saw is an indication
that there is no place the heart cannot reach. And since there is no
place the heart cannot reach it cannot really be left to stray.

Q. When the Great Sage is in the World of the Ancients he is Beautiful
Lady Yü. How does he become so lovely? In the World of the Future,
he is King Yama of Hell. How does he become so fearsome?

A. When the heart goes into the future, it is in a most precarious situation. If one doesn't fortify his spirit he is sure to be utterly defeated.
By exterminating the Six Thieves, Monkey expelled evil. Punishing
Ch'in Kuei established his direction. In paying respect to Yüeh Fei
he returned to the right. This is basically how the Great Sage broke
out of the Demon Desire.

Q. When the Great Sage is in the Emerald Green World, he sees that
the T'ang Priest is a general. Why?

A. There is no need to discuss this. You need only see the nine words
on his banner: "The Supreme and Venerable Commander for
Wiping out Desire."

---

[4] The T'ang dynasty (A.D. 618–907) and the Sung dynasty (A.D. 960–1279).

Q. In the thirteenth chapter, the T'ang Priest weeps in Crying Ospreys Hall while the girl playing the *p'i-p'a* sings her song. There is a heavy feeling of mournful wind and bitter rain.

A. The roots of desire in this world can be summed up in one word: "sorrow."

Q. The Great Sage suddenly has a wife and children. How can this be?

A. Dream thoughts are upside-down.

Q. When the Great Sage emerges from the Demon of Desire, there is the chaos of the five colored banners. Why is this?

A. The *Purity Sūtra* says that when chaos runs its course, there is a return to the root. When desire reaches its extremity, you see your own nature.

Q. When the Great Sage comes across peonies, he immediately enters the Demon of Desire. When he fights in the vanguard rushing the enemy's barricades, he immediately escapes desire. Why is this?

A. In killing desire, one must be prepared to cut it in half with a single stroke.

Q. Can one really gouge holes in heaven?

A. Here is the author's intention: If the Great Sage hadn't encountered the men who dug holes in heaven, he could never have entered the Demon of Desire.

Q. In the original *Journey to the West*, the monsters all have the heads of cows and tigers, make noises like a jackal, or glare like a wolf. Now in the first fifteen chapters of *The Tower of Myriad Mirrors*, the descriptions of the Ch'ing Fish show it to be young and delicate, almost human. How is this?

A. Your four words—young, delicate, almost human—precisely describe the shape this foremost demon has assumed since the beginning of time.

CHINESE NAMES & TERMS

An Lu-shan 安祿山

Ch'an (Zen) 禪
Chang Chieh 張
Chang Ch'iu 張丘
Chang Chün 張俊
Chang Fei 張飛
Chang Han 章邯
Chang Hsien 張憲
Chang Liang 張良
Ch'ang O 嫦娥
Chao (Sung royal family name) 趙
Chao Ch'eng 趙成
Chen-chiang 鎮江
Ch'en Hsüan-tsang 陳玄奘
Ch'i (state of) 齊
Ch'i Li-chi 綺里季
Ch'i Po 岐伯
Ch'i Ch'ung-li 綦崇禮
Chieh (ruler of Hsia) 桀
chieh (a tea from Ch'ang-hsing County, Chekiang Province) 岕
chih (musical mode) 徵
Chin (dynasty) 金
Ch'in (dynasty) 秦
Chin (dynasty) 晉
Ch'in Kuei 秦檜
Chin P'ing Mei 金瓶梅
Chin-t'ou Mountain 金頭山
ch'ing (desire) 情
Ch'ing (dynasty) 清
Ch'ing Fish (demon) 鯖魚精
Ching K'o 荊軻
Ch'ing-kuo fu-jen 傾國夫人
Ching River 涇水

Chou (ruler of Shang) 紂
Chou (dynasty) 周
Ch'u (state of) 楚
Chu Hsiao-chi 祝小姬
Chu Wu-neng 豬悟能
Chuang-tzu 莊子

Fan Li 范蠡
Fan Tseng 范增
fu 賦
Fu-ch'ai (king of Wu) 夫差
Fu-hsi 伏羲

Han (dynasty) 漢
Han Chüeh 寒爵
Han Kao-tsu 漢高祖
Ho Chu 何鑄
Hou I 后羿
Hsi-shih 西施
"Hsi-tz'u" 繫辭
Hsi-yu chi 西遊記
Hsi-yu pu 西遊補
Hsia-huang 夏黃
Hsiang, King of Ch'u 楚湘王
Hsiang River 湘江
Hsiang Yü 項羽
Hsiao (river) 瀟
Hsien-yang 咸陽
Hsü 徐
Hsü Yu 許由
Hsüan, King of Chou 周宣王
Hsüan-tsang 玄奘
Hsüan-wu 玄武
Hsüan-yüan 軒轅
Hua K'uei 花夔

137

Huai-su 懷素
Huang Chang 黃章
Huang Tao-chou 黃道周
Hun-tun 混沌
Hung-lou meng 紅樓夢

I Ching 易經
I River 易水

Ju-lin wai-shih 儒林外史

Kao San-ch'u 高三楚
Kao-t'ang 高唐
Kao-tsung 高宗
Kao Wei-ming 高未明
Ko-ch'iang-hua 隔牆花
Ko-t'ien (king) 葛天
Kou-ch'en 鉤陳
Kou-chien (king of Yüeh) 勾踐
Kuan-yin 觀音
k'uei (hexagram) 暌
k'un (hexagram) 困
K'un-lun Mountains 崑崙山
k'ung ch'ing neng ching 空青能淨
Kung-sun 公孫

Lao-tzu 老子
Li (T'ang royal family name) 李
Li (court of) 黎
Li Chien-ch'eng 李建成
Li K'uang 李曠
"Li-sao" 離騷
Li Shih-min 李世民
Li Ssu 李斯
Li Yüan-chi 李元吉
Lin Ta-chieh 林大節
Ling (king of Ch'u) 靈
Ling-chi (bodhisattva) 靈吉
Liu Ch'un 柳春
Liu Fu 劉復
Liu Pang 劉邦
Liu Po-ch'in 劉伯欽
Liu Ta-chieh 劉大杰
Liu Yü 劉豫

Lo (river) 洛
Lu-li 角里
Lü I-hao 呂頤浩

Ming (dynasty) 明
mo hsü yu 莫須有
Mo-ch'i Hsieh 万候尚
Mo-t'an-lang 摸檀郎
Mt. Heng 衡山
Mt. Heng 恆山
Mt. Hua 華山
Mt. Li 驪山
Mt. Shang 商山
Mt. Sung 嵩山
Mt. T'ai 泰山
Mu-ch'a 木叉
Mu Ch'ao-nan 木巢南

Nü-kua 女媧

P'an-ku 盤古
P'ei 沛
Pei-chuan-p'ing-t'ing 背轉娉婷
P'eng 蓬
pi-i bird 比翼
p'i-p'a 琵琶
pien-chih (musical mode) 變徵
P'ing-hsiang 蘋香

San-kuo yen-i 三國演義
Shan-yang 山陽
Shang (dynasty) 商
Shao-hsing (reign period) 紹興
Shen Ching-nan 沈敬南
Shih-chieh shu-chü 世界書局
Shih Ching 詩經
Shih Ch'ung 石崇
Shih Mei-ch'iu 石媚
Shu (state of) 蜀
Shui-hu chuan 水滸傳
Shun (sage ruler) 舜
Sui (dynasty) 隋
Sui Yang-ti 隋煬帝
Sun Wen-wei 孫文蔚

Sun Wu-huan 孫悟幻
Sun Wu-k'ung 孫悟空
Sun Yü 孫虞
Sung (dynasty) 宋
Sung-feng (road) 嵩封
Sung I 宋義
Sung-lo 松蘿
Sung T'ai-tsu 宋太祖

Ta-lan 撻懶
T'ai-hua 太華
T'ai-k'un (pond) 太昆
Tan (prince of Yen) 丹
T'ang (dynasty) 唐
t'ang (sugar) 糖
T'ang Hsüan-tsung 唐玄宗
T'ang T'ai-tsung 唐太宗
Teng Chung
Ts'ao Ts'ao 曹操
Tseng Shen 曾參
Ts'ui Chüeh 崔珏
tui (trigram) 兌
t'ung (tree) 桐
Tung Cho 董卓
Tung-t'ing (lake) 洞庭
Tung-yüan 東園
Tung Yüeh 董說, style Jo-yü 若雨
tz'u 辭
Tzu-ying (king of Ch'in) 子嬰

Wang Chün 王俊
Wang Kuei 王貴
Wang Lun 王倫
Wei 魏
Wei Cheng 魏徵
Wen-hsüeh ku-chi k'an-hsing-she 文學古籍
 刊行社
Wu (state of) 吳
Wu Ch'eng-en 吳承恩
Wu-ch'i-mai 吳乞買
Wu-ching 悟淨
Wu-ch'ing 悟青
Wu-huai 無懷
Wu, King 武王

Wu Mountain 巫山
Wu-neng 悟能
Wu, Han Emperor 漢武帝
Wu-chu (Chin general) 兀术
wu-t'ung (tree) 梧桐
Wu Tzu-hsü 伍子胥
Wu Yu 烏有

Yang Kuei-fei 楊貴妃
Yao (sage ruler) 堯
Yen (state of) 燕
Yama 閻羅
Young Shen 沈郎
yü (musical mode) 羽
Yü (sage ruler) 禹
Yü, Beautiful Lady 虞美人
Yü Shun 虞舜
Yü Sun 虞孫
Yüeh (state of) 越
Yüeh Fei 岳飛
Yün-meng Marshes 雲夢澤

Afterword

We should like to take the opportunity of this ebook conversion to briefly address the questions that have been raised regarding the author of *The Tower of Myriad Mirrors*. This short novel was first printed in 1641, under the authorship of "Master of the Studio for Quiet Whistling" (Ching-hsiao-chai chu-ren 靜嘯齋主人) who was also named as the writer of the "Answers to the Questions (on the work)" that we appended to our translation. Since the second half of the 17th century, Master of the Studio for Quiet Whistling has largely been identified as Tung Yüeh 董説. The Chinese character for this author's given name has always been read "Yüeh" by modern scholars, even though it can also be read "Shuo," "Shui," and "T'o" depending on its meanings in different contexts. In a 2006 publication entitled *Studies on the Ming Loyalist Tung T'o* (Ming i-min tung t'o yen-chiu 明遺民董説研究), Professor Zhao Hongjuan 趙紅娟 offers convincing evidence that our author's name should be pronounced "Tung T'o." We agree with Professor Zhao's analysis; however, we have maintained "Tung Yüeh" for the author's name to avoid confusion vis-a-vis previous editions.

The authorship of this novel has been a matter of dispute among scholars of Chinese fiction since 1985 when Gao Hongjun 高洪鈞 published an article in which he challenged the traditional view and argued that Tung T'o's father Tung Ssu-chang 董斯張 wrote the book because "Quiet Whistling" was the name of his studio. Gao's argument was immediately contested by Feng Baoshan 馮保善 and Xu Jiang 徐江 who argued that Tung Ssu-chang had never used "Master of the Studio for Quiet Whistling" as a pseudonym, and that there was no taboo in late Ming against a son using his father's studio name as part of his own pseudonym. In her 2006 book, Zhao Hongjuan presents an abundance of evidence from various sources including the novel itself to reconfirm that Tung T'o is the author. Nonetheless, in the introduction to his 2011 publication *A Supplement to Journey to the West with Textual Criticism and Commentary* (Hsi-yu pu chiao-chu 西遊補校注), Professor Li Qiancheng 李前程 continued to support Gao's argument by critiquing some details in the counter argument and advancing what he felt to be proofs of Tung Ssu-chang's authorship from the latter's writings.

The first edition of our translation was published in 1978. It should be noted that when we were revising that translation in preparation for the 2000 second edition, we were fully aware of the dispute in the authorship of this novel. But after reviewing all of the arguments and evidence presented by scholars involved in the debate, we decided to continue the traditional designation of Tung T'o as the author. We came to this decision chiefly because we felt that the advocates of Tung Ssu-chang's authorship had not correctly understood a key piece of evidence: Tung T'o's own reference to having written the novel. This reference is expressed in a couplet in one of ten poems written in 1650 under the group title of "Random Thoughts" (*Man-hsing shih* 漫興詩): "*Journey to the West*--I have supplemented it with (my own) fictional writing: / I return to the empty Tower of Myriad Mirrors, having passed the Provincial Examination." （西遊曾補虞初筆，萬鏡樓空及第歸） Tung T'o also added a personal note to these lines, saying, "Ten years ago, I wrote a 'supplement' to *Journey to the West*, (in which) there is the episode of 'The Tower of Myriad Mirrors.'" （自注云：余十年前曾補西遊，有萬鏡樓一則。）

As Xu Jiang has well argued, Tung T'o's writing of the novel in 1640 had much to do with his sense of bitterness and disappointment over his failure of passing the Provincial Examination (*hsiang-shih* 鄉試) one year earlier--the author's satirical treatment of Civil Service Examination in Chapter 4 that begins the depiction of the Tower of Myriad Mirrors clearly supports this observation. Apart from this event in his life, we simply could not believe that Tung T'o's couplet and note, given the way he has phrased them, can be taken, as Gao Hongjun and his followers have done, to mean that *Journey to the West* （西遊） refers to *A Supplement to Journey to the West* （西遊補） by his father, and that he himself has only written or "supplemented" one episode or chapter to his father's work.

We are happy to report that Zhao Hongjuan has completed an article in which she brings her expertise on late Ming and early Ch'ing literature to bear on Tung T'o's authorship, reviews all theories, arguments, and evidence, and presents what we believe will be the decisive conclusion to the controversy. Her article is expected to appear in print in a scholarly journal soon.

We used the Wade-Giles system of romanization for Chinese names and terms in our 1978 translation because it was standard practice at the time. For practical reasons, we have not departed from Wade-Giles in subsequent editions, including this ebook.

Shuen-fu Lin
Larry J. Schulz

June 2012